THE SUPERSTITIOUS ROMANCE

MILLIONAIRE ROMANCE

ANASTASIA ALEXANDER

THE SUPERSTITIOUS ROMANCE

ANASTASIA ALEXANDER

ELEGANT ELEPHANT BOOKS

The Superstitious Romance

Published by Elegant Elephant

Copyright © 2020 by Anastasia Alexander

Cover and ebook design by Molly Philipps

ISBN:

Printed in the United States of America

Year of first printing: 2014

BOOKS BY ANASTASIA ALEXANDER
MILLIONAIRE ROMANCE SERIES

To Rick: my champion, supporter, and best friend.
And to Anna and Lexi: thank you for all your love, laughter, and delight you
bring to my life. May you always be happy.

CHAPTER ONE

The pale blue sky took on the same hue as his eyes, a deceptively calming color Camille Marie Britain had gazed at for twenty-six years of marriage. Now she saw the color when the sky decided to torture her with painful memories. If she could dab it with a paintbrush to change the hue, she would. It didn't matter what tint as long as it wasn't his color, anything but his. She wanted nothing around to remind her of his infectious laugh, the way he spun rhetoric, or his charismatic charm.

That's why she had fled her house and her job to come to God's favorite land: Island Park, Idaho. And here she was, meditating on a wooden dock being gently rocked by boat waves, surrounded by purple mountains and crisp, cool air with a hint of stale algae. The setting sun spread a thin, pencil stripe of lavender across the green valley. This sacred hideaway exuded a magnificent peace. The perfect place to run to. She shut her eyes to better concentrate.

The October breeze picked up by the time Camille finished her deep breathing meditation on the dock by the lake. Slowly, as she was trained, she opened her eyes to see pine trees and ruffled waves—and then looked east as a dark object caught her eye. What was it? A pine tree? No, it was too close to the shoreline. Driftwood? Maybe, but it sure would be a big one. The object seemed to move. She watched, now intrigued. The shadow moved between the pine lodge trees and the licking waves of the lake. A deer? Dog? Moose? She made out what might be a head, arms. Perhaps Gaia, goddess of Earth, was coming to bless her. But no, she could now see a hat, boots, and a bulky form.

She drew her legs close, sitting in a round ball. A man. Only one cabin away. She fumbled with the old wood underneath her hand until a sliver broke away from the board. She twisted the shard between her fingers as she realized the shadow, person, man was coming toward her. It wasn't long before the stranger's footsteps clicked against the dock. The evening swallowed up most of his physical features, but he was larger than she'd expected, a solid giant, with a broad, wide chest, lean stomach, and long, sturdy legs anchored by black cowboy boots. But what caught her attention and caused her to scoot back was the hatchet in the sheath on his belt and the rifle slung over his shoulder.

"Howdy," boomed his voice, deep and masculine. "Do you know why there's a light in that cabin?" He motioned to the front of the cabin, which faced the dock.

"No," she muttered, hating the interest that flared through her. He was a man, and that was all she needed to know to stay clear.

"The Clarks asked me to keep an eye on the place. Someone's moving around in there. I'm going to check it out."

"We . . . we're renting the cabin." Her eyes focused on the hatchet.

"Oh, I thought you said . . . never mind. If you're the renters, then we're neighbors." He leaned over, his hand extended. "I live several cabins that-a-way." He pointed into the darkness from which he'd emerged as he grabbed her cold hand, enveloping it with his large, firm grip. "I'm Jackson Armstrong. And you are?"

His gaze burned into her as she prayed a silent thanks for the mask of darkness and the fact that his attentions seemed amicable. "Camille."

"Camille, what?"

"Britain," she said, wishing she didn't always answer every question anyone asked.

"Mom, phone." Her eighteen-year-old daughter jogged down the dock, waving a cordless phone. Darlene's bouncing honey-brown hair reached her waist and delicately framed her pale face. She had a small, catlike nose and fragile cheekbones, which matched nicely with her slender frame. She'd inherited the best traits of both parents. Unfortunately, that included her father's haunting pale blue eyes—eyes impossible to avoid.

"Darlene, our neighbor, Jackson." Camille gestured toward him.

They shook hands, and then the fellow sidled off the dock. "Better be headin' home. Just came to check the cabin," he called out before disappearing into the trees. He whistled a tune Camille didn't recognize.

"He's a good whistler," Darlene said.

Camille shook her head. "Don't you try it. Whistling is always a bad omen when women do it. You wouldn't want to be responsible for summoning misfortune." She didn't really believe that, of course, but she had enough problems with bad luck, and she planned to do everything she could to ward it away during her stay here.

———

"You wouldn't want to be responsible . . . responsible . . . responsible . . ." Water splashed on Jackson's boots as the woman's fading words reverberated through him. Mothers were the same everywhere. Pouring guilt and orders on their kids: do this, do that, don't ever . . . Mothers believed that if they didn't tell their children to breathe, they'd forget to. He knew his mother had done it—and still did it—out of love, but it was irritating all the same. The way he learned to deal with it was to love her, accept her, and most of the time, overlook her flaws.

The lady he had just met, although attractive in a smart, intelligent way, seemed to be extra endowed with this cautioning business if she took it as far as a superstition of whistling. What utter and complete

3

nonsense. It was hard to believe the world had been in the enlightened age for centuries and people still took stock in that hocus pocus stuff. That was why he would stay away from women and remain alone in nature—no more answering to a female.

He had made it to the dirt path that headed up to his cabin, where snarling weeds had overgrown most of the trail. He'd have to clear it. Maybe tomorrow. He also needed to get his photography assignment done. Not much time for motorcycling on the back roads. He shouldn't have agreed to play handyman for Mrs. Clark. Now he would have to deal with Camille and all the demands an upper-class woman would require. But he couldn't say no to Mrs. Clark with her cancer returning, especially with her family being so non-supportive. There was a woman who wouldn't nag children, if she had them. She was too stalwart for that.

Miserable luck that she'd rented to an academic woman. *But maybe I'm getting carried away*, he thought as he knelt by his stone fire pit and checked the fish in his Dutch oven. *She might not be that bad.*

Not that he cared, of course.

The trout looked done. Too bad he hadn't put potatoes and carrots in for a complete meal. Or didn't have any lemon and salt to flavor the fish. A woman would have thought about all those extra things before even catching the fish.

His mind wandered back to the woman with eyes so deep he'd felt he could drown in them. Maybe Camille's husband would do all the repairs himself. He stared at the flavorless fish with a frown. Maybe he would wander over there around dinnertime and score a decent meal. He carried the Dutch oven into his cabin, and the stink that had formed in the bathroom even overwhelmed the smell of the fish. He couldn't ignore it much longer. His bathroom had become so dirty he feared getting athlete's foot.

He ate his fish in silence with none of the endless chatter he was used to enduring when his ex-wife had been around. She sure could ramble on, sounding like the school teacher on Charlie Brown, "Whaaa, whaaa, whaaa." After scraping the last bit of meat off the bones, he dumped the remnants into the trash, put his plate in the sink, and flipped on the radio to listen to a talk show. He'd have to straighten up the cabin before his son came. He wanted no reports going back the other way that his new, simpler life had any flaws in it.

———

Why did that man have to come over? Camille thought, reluctantly taking the phone from Darlene's hand. And why had someone called? She wanted to be left alone. Completely alone, all but for Darlene. Camille needed time to heal, to figure out who she was now that she was no longer Mrs. Adam Britain. She didn't want to be social and neighborly. "Hello," she snapped into the phone.

"Run into any bears?" her oldest son asked.

"I'm reading a survivalist handbook right now."

"Great. I can see it. You go on a walk and stumble across an angry black bear and say, 'Bear, can you wait a minute while I look up what I'm supposed to do in my survivalist handbook?'"

"Relax. I know what to do. You put your hands above your head and walk around pretending that's how tall you are. Take bear-fear off your list."

"Mom, you're not taking me seriously."

"Would you relax? I'm fine."

"But tomorrow's Halloween—"

Her son talked on, but she didn't listen. Instead, she noticed a chill spreading through her. Her son did have reason to worry. Ever since she studied folklore for her minor in college, strange, uncomfortable things happened to her. She had broken her arm twice on previous Halloweens and her leg once on Friday the thirteenth. "You're one crazy woman," her husband had told her many times. "You know you bring the accidents on yourself, don't you? No one else has these things happen to them. You make them happen on purpose to prove yourself right."

She knew differently.

"Richard," she broke into her son's endless stream of concern, "I will be extra careful. You have no need to worry."

5

"Well, okay. I'll call tomorrow to see if I need to fly out. 'Til then," he said.

She sighed. Her son had turned into her father—an over-protective version. "Darlene," she called to the end of the dock, where her daughter stood looking over the lake. "Let's go in. It's getting dark."

Together they hiked the incline to the tiny, lodge-pole pine cabin she'd rented for the semester. She flung the door open as if she owned the place and was used to coming in and out, but the illusion of the paradise being a familiar home stopped there. She shivered, pulling her wool sweater tighter around her prickling skin.

She checked the thermostat. "Darlene, stay away from that Jackson person."

"He seemed nice." Her daughter's matchmaking skills were apparently shifting into gear. "Good looking too."

"Just don't. Please." Camille gave her plea more thought, then added, "Forget I said anything. Let's make hot chocolate. Help me find the kitchen supply box."

"I can't believe we're out here in the middle of nowhere."

"You're the one who begged to come." Camille searched the cupboards for a teapot.

"I couldn't miss seeing my mom on a wild adventure. You never know, we might run into a bear."

The two fell into pleasant chatter until they grew tired and dragged themselves up the creaky stairs to their bedrooms. Camille had taken the smaller room that smelled of pine from all the pine furniture—a large bed covered with a checkered handmade quilt, a rocking chair, and a chest of drawers topped with a lamp that cast a glow of light onto the log walls. A pine closet graced the opposite side of the room. If Camille had brought up her suitcase, it would have filled the space between the chest of drawers, the rocking chair, the closet, and the bed. The cozy room invited her to snuggle into the blankets, studying a book about Yellowstone until sleep consumed her, but she must have left her book in the kitchen.

Not wanting to disturb Darlene, who had left her bedroom door open, Camille crept down the stairs without flipping on the hallway light. As she moved down the stairs, an uneasiness seemed to crawl over her like thousands of spiders dancing on her skin. To add to her nerves, the wind had picked up outside, sending a howl echoing through the cabin. Camille stumbled around the unpacked boxes in the hall, the clock light on the microwave guiding her. Eleven forty-six. Only fourteen minutes until Halloween. Seizing her book from the counter, she hurried to her bed.

She managed to almost fall asleep, but then suddenly she sat up in bed, startled. "Was that the hoot of an owl?" she asked the quiet room. Another cry came. "It must be an owl."

The lamplight flicked. A blanket-wrapped Darlene rushed into the room. "Did you hear that?"

"Yes."

"That's a bad sign."

"I know."

"What are owl cries supposed to mean?" Darlene asked. She shivered as she sat on the foot of the bed. "I forget."

"The Romans and Native Americans thought they signaled death and disaster," Camille said. "But Greeks liked owls because it was Athena's bird. They thought anything associated with an owl brought wisdom."

"I like the Greek version better than the Romans'," Darlene said.

Camille nodded as another screech filled the air. "I'll take the Greek interpretation too. We just have to make sure the bird doesn't come in or fly around our house. Because if it does . . ."

"What?" Darlene asked.

"It's a death omen."

"Oh." Her daughter pulled the blanket over her head. "We're being silly," she said.

"I've studied too much about superstitious traditions," Camille agreed.

"The problem is that superstitions sometimes have legitimacy."

"I know. Either this getaway already has a bad omen cast on it, or we'll be blessed with wisdom."

"I hope this is Athena's owl."

"I do too." Camille couldn't help but think that if she were here with a man, she would feel a lot less nervous. She was being silly. She shouldn't need a man around to feel safe.

The owl hooted again as they shook under their blankets, and Camille pulled hers tighter around her chest. If Jackson were here, he wouldn't be afraid of the hoot of the owl. Instead, he would most likely make fun of her silliness. No way would he let those things bother him. But then, he seemed to be the kind of guy who didn't let much get to him.

CHAPTER TWO

The whole separation and divorce had been too normal, too calm—surreal. Camille had been sitting at her cherry wood desk grading papers. The stack was thick and soaring. That's what she remembered most clearly—how high the "to grade" pile was, as if someone was seeing how tall the paper tower could go before it tumbled.

Adam had come into her office. She had felt his presence, his command over her and her time, and had resisted the order for her attention. She was angry, depressed, and in a withdrawn state of mind, feeling neglected from his long absences. If he'd finally come to his senses and realized he missed her, he'd have to work at recapturing her affection.

She didn't have to look up to know how he would look. She could see every detail in her mind. He'd be clothed in a ridiculously expensive suit, which he'd always managed to keep wrinkle-free. His bleached blond, wavy hair would be in place—except for the cowlick on the right side of his forehead that would stubbornly poke up no matter the amount of gel. His weather-beaten skin would have a brown tint from hours spent on the tennis courts and golf courses. His cruel mouth would be drawn thin and stern in disapproval, emphasized by the pencil-line blond mustache that shadowed his upper lip.

"Camille." He had spoken in a surprisingly normal tone as if sensing none of the built-up tension between them. She made a checkmark on the paper she was grading. "Yes."

"When you get a chance, I need you to look over these papers and tell me what you think."

She extended her hand to take them from him and set them on the pile, her attention back on the essay.

"Aren't you going to see what it is?" he asked.

"It's on my pile," she mumbled.

He left without a word.

If it had been a normal day, her curiosity would have prompted her to stop her schoolwork and hurry to find out what he'd given her. But it wasn't a normal day, and she was in an extremely stubborn mood, not wanting to be rushed into anything she wasn't ready for. She took her time grading the paper. She went over the words with the intensity of a scientist searching for a new organism. The poor soul's paper was blood red with her ink by the time she finished. After writing an F at the top of the page, she picked up the legal papers her husband had left. Surprisingly, her hand was steady and her pulse calm, regular. It took a moment for her to realize it was a divorce complaint and stipulation. She eyed a few more pages and then set it aside. She would grade that after she had gone through all the essays that needed her attention.

This memory remained in her mind as she sat up in bed. Dreaming about it last night left a desperate quality, not like the real event. In her dream, she felt panicky, her heart raced, and a tremble went through her. She lacked the calm composure she'd had in reality. She struggled to block the dream and the desire to sob. It was then she grew cold, very cold. She tugged on her blanket to pull it up around her, but the quilt barely moved. Her eyes adjusting to the early dawn, she detected something lying at the end of the bed. The shadow moved and gave a faint sigh. The sigh was short and light like a kitten purring, giving a familiar feeling of happy days gone by. Her shoulders slumped in relief. Darlene.

Camille slipped her stiff legs out of bed, the icy floor teasing her feet. Hopping onto the braided rug in the middle of the room, she paused to release a deep breath, fogging the air. "Geez, it's cold," she muttered, sliding the thermostat to ninety on her way out. The cabin's chill wrapped around her as she flipped on the hall light. What she needed was a fire. She had never made one, but it couldn't be too hard.

Before worrying about that, she strolled to the window. Dawn struggled to break through the thick mist that swarmed over the vegetation. As she watched, letting the tranquil environment soothe the raw pain of the nightmare, someone suddenly slipped from the fog, the person still far enough away that she saw no distinctive features. The form approached swiftly, and soon Camille could detect that the early morning walker carried something long and slender. It could be a cane, a stick, or a . . . a . . . hatchet.

She didn't stay in front of the window to discover what it was. Instead, she got into her jeans and flannel shirt, scrubbed a toothbrush over her teeth, and pulled a comb through her hair. That done, she hustled to start the fire. Unfortunately, the wood box was empty. She hurried outside, the dying, hip-high weeds depositing dew on her pants as she passed by on her way to the wood stack.

She halted her pace, spying a man standing next to the log pile, whistling. Jackson, the man from the day before. Camille folded her arms neatly over her chest, approaching him. Today Jackson wore a cap and had at least two days' growth of stubble on his face, giving him a wild, hardy appearance. She suspected the roughness would dissolve almost completely with a good shave. His firm, square jaw told of decisiveness and strength, yet his full cheeks hinted of vulnerability. His eyes, a deep chocolate color, showed a kind of hurt—or was it coldness? He possessed an attractiveness she couldn't understand, but he didn't appear to have an intellect she could admire.

"Good mornin'." His voice rang out like a brass bell. "I just came to chop yer wood. I noticed the stack was low last night."

She nodded, lifting a few logs in her arms, and then sensed her actions might be taken as rude. "I appreciate your offer, but you don't need to bother. We've got it all under control."

"That's all right, ma'am." He put a log onto the chopping block. "This is what I'm paid for."

She glanced at his square, stubborn chin. There was no use fighting him. She could see that right off. She gave up and started for the cabin, her arms heavy with logs.

"Let me get that for you." He rested the hatchet against the remaining stack.

She resisted, not wanting to depend on any man again for anything, especially not a man that attractive. "No, that's quite all right. I'm building a fire."

"I'll do it for you." He reached for the logs in her hands.

She adjusted the logs, keeping hold of them, and was going to say, "No thanks," but instead, a short, stifled yelp slipped out as a sliver shot deep into her index finger.

"Are you all right?" he asked.

She automatically stepped back, seeing worry on his face—or maybe curiosity. "Fine." Balancing the logs, she dashed for the back door, which she fumbled to open as she felt the weight of his deep brown eyes. Heat rushed to her face. She gave an extra tug on the doorknob, and a log slipped from her arms, falling squarely on the upper part of her foot. She gasped, hobbled over the log, and shut the cabin door to suffer the pain in privacy. Soon afterward, she dragged herself into the living room, wondering if Jackson would watch for smoke to come out of the chimney. If so, she aimed to quench any doubt he might harbor of her inadequacies.

It didn't take her long to lay the logs in a closely stacked pile and form a pyramid design inside the grating. She found the three remaining matches. The first broke while striking it against the stones of the fireplace. The second took two tries to ignite, but the flame disappeared as fast as it ignited. Camille held up the last match and considered using lighter fluid. Grabbing her sweater, she headed to the garage to search for some. A brutally cold gust of wind greeted her, followed by the dust of the garage. She fumbled through dirty bottles, fishing poles, and old shoes. Wiping the muck from her fingers, she eyed a plastic bottle on top of a cabinet in the far corner. She climbed the shelf, disturbing the stale dust covering everything. Her nose twitched with a sneeze. She scrunched her nose and held the sneeze in as her grasp tightened on the shelf.

The next thing she knew, she was on the floor, the rotting shelf having given way when she sneezed. Checking to see if she had injured herself, she thought of her son Richard's comment about calling tomorrow to see if he needed to fly out. She sighed. He had once admired his mother, proud of her ability to take on those "Big windbags," as he called her colleagues. Camille liked making her courses more interactive, cross-disciplinary, and hands-on, but doing so had caused a lot of static in the department. Every time Camille stood up for her ideas, she'd tell her son, loving to see his pride in his strong-willed mom.

This had changed since the divorce. She felt rejected. Disposed of. Disillusioned. How could she continue? Was her success as a teacher and mother an illusion also?

She brushed dust from her hands. Now even Richard, her former supporter, doubted her. He was becoming like Adam. She bit her lower lip. Just like his father! In fact, before Adam left, he made sure she knew how he regarded her. "You're weak, and that revolts me," he'd said. She remembered that moment well. She had gathered his clothes, thrown them on the floor, and sat on top of the pile like an angry queen bee. When Adam pulled his pants from under her, she frantically grabbed a shirt and clutched it. Adam stared at her with empty eyes, cocking his chin to the left, saying nothing.

He tossed his pants to the floor with such an air of disgust: lips drawn tight and straight, his mustache forming a line above his thin lips, his circular eyes narrowed into dark brewing clouds, and his cheeks puffed into two huge sour balls. Camille knew this horrid image would never leave her. He, however, did leave. He stood there, letting his disgust seep into her before turning away from her and the pile and slipping out the side door, never to return.

His sickened response to her desperate childish reaction to clutch onto all they had built, all they had shared, all the promised potential, made her realize Adam did not know her. He didn't have the faintest flicker of understanding. He may have lived with her for twenty-six years, but he reeked of ignorance. He had committed the fatal flaw of thinking her love was a weakness. Someday, Adam would understand that she was strong, sturdy, and most of all, tenacious. Then the regret and realization of what he had done would hit him. To prove her self-reliance, she had come to the wilderness. The first test of her ability to survive on her own would be to build a fire. She already had two strikes against her—dropping a log on her foot and falling from a shelf made two accidents. Superstition again. One more self-wounding injury to go; accidents always came in threes. She hoped she'd get the third one over soon and that it wouldn't be too painful. She wiped her dusty hands on her pant leg and stood when the garage side door opened. Camille didn't have to look to know Jackson filled the doorway.

"I heard a crash," his deep voice boomed. "Everything all right?"

"No problems," she muttered as she climbed a sturdy shelf. She snatched the lighter fluid and hurried by this nosy neighbor at whom she wanted to shout, "Go away!" She almost made it to the cabin when she noticed that she hadn't grabbed lighter fluid after all; it was brake fluid. The thought of returning to the garage to face Jackson's amused eyes made her flush. She charged on to find she had to tug on the back door again to get inside. Hoping that he had, in fact, left, she gave an extra firm push. To her horror, as the door swung open, a brown squirrel bumped against her leg and headed straight into the cabin. "Oh, no, you don't!" she yelled at the animal, hobbling after him. "Get out of here, you disease-spreading rodent."

"What in Hades is going on here?"

She turned to see her daughter's sleep-droopy eyes and tousled hair. "Help me get this squirrel out of here fast," Camille said.

"What?"

"A squirrel's in the living room," she said. "Help me chase it out."

"No way."

"Darlene."

"No. That's gross. You do it."

"Come with me then," Camille said. "And I mean it. No lip. We have to get it out of here, or I'll never be able to concentrate on my book. It's like living with a mouse. I'll go absolutely crazy."

"I know, Mom. We've done that before. Remember?" She followed her mother into the living room. "You screamed at all times of the day, whenever he decided to . . ."

The squirrel was perched on the couch, his eyes focused. It took several seconds before the shock wore off Darlene and she screamed loud and full. The creature darted behind the couch.

"Get a broom," Camille said. Darlene hurried into the kitchen while Camille tried to coax confidence into herself, fast. She felt as if there were a hidden camera watching her, betraying her every step to Richard and Adam and perhaps that Jackson guy. She wouldn't prove them right.

Her heart pounded loud, rapid, and strong as she peeked under the couches and chairs, filled with fear that the squirrel would latch onto her face any second. It didn't take long for her to find the creature hiding beneath the plaid couch along the south wall. The beady eyes of the squirrel darted around in acute awareness of the danger surrounding him. Camille's eyes connected with the creature's for a brief, unnerving second. She stifled a scream, fighting her revulsion. Immediately she set to work building a barricade with the moving boxes, but unfortunately, all that served to do was give the squirrel an obstacle course to exercise in. He made it through the obstacles and darted straight behind the refrigerator.

"It'll chew the wires and start a fire," Camille said to Darlene, straining to move the brown refrigerator. "Help me."

"Move away," Darlene said. "Let muscle woman go to work." She flexed her biceps, grabbed the appliance, and rocked it from the wall. The squirrel ran for the space between the oven and the cupboard. Darlene flexed once more and moved the stove, only to have the squirrel dash upstairs.

"Our rooms!" Darlene yelled.

Camille sat on the dining room bench and asked, "What can he hurt up there?"

"I don't want to share my bed."

"I say we give up until we get back from the store," Camille said. "We can ask how to get rid of it there. All we're doing now is making a big mess." They looked around the place, scattered with boxes, clothes, pans, and the out-of-place oven and refrigerator. Darlene slumped onto the stairs. Camille hunted for the last match. She held it up. "Ready for the toasty fire?"

"More than ever."

Camille struck the match, and after three tries it flared. The fire raged on top of the log but died once the paper vanished.

Both of them groaned. "We'll go to the store for lighter fluid and matches after breakfast." Camille forced cheer into her words while rummaging through boxes until she found the oatmeal. "You can go back to sleep if you like, dear."

"Why don't you get that guy Jackson to come and make us a fire? I bet he could fix the broken heater, too."

Nervous tension flushed through Camille. "We know nothing about him. Besides, I can do it myself. So what's the verdict? Bed or store?"

"Go for a walk to the cabin a little ways down from here and ask for help."

"Enough of that." Camille took a long breath before asking, "Bed or store?"

"I want to see what a country store is like," Darlene answered.

"You want adventure, do you?" Camille arched her eyebrows, relieved to change the subject.

Darlene laughed. "Anything will be an adventure if I'm in the same state as you on Halloween or Friday the Thirteenth. Lucky me gets to have both holidays less than two weeks apart."

"So you do know about that?"

"How could I not know with Richard raving on as he does," Darlene said.

"Richard." Camille sighed. "Sometimes, he worries me." Her efforts to scoot the stove toward the wall failed, and Darlene jumped up to help her.

When they finished, Camille ushered her daughter away, knowing how long it took her to get ready. Camille would have breakfast cooked before Darlene was halfway done. She placed a pot of water on the stove, glad that it was electric, and decided to start the fire by lighting a paper with the stove burner. Shaking her head in dismay, she wondered why she hadn't thought of it before. She blackened several pieces of paper, but each spark died without producing a flame. She twisted more paper and put it against the burner. Still nothing. Maybe the dampness of the wood prevented a fire from starting. She set the logs out along the hearth to dry.

Darlene came out of the bathroom with a tube of foundation in her hand. "Mom, why is thirteen considered unlucky?"

"People say it's 'cause there were thirteen people present at the Last Supper. But the fear of thirteen was around long before that. Romans believed it symbolized death, destruction, and misfortune."

"What does the Friday have to do with it?" Darlene asked.

"I'm not sure. All I could learn about it was that Friday, May Thirteenth, was the worst day to get married."

Darlene returned to caking on her makeup, and Camille searched for a loaf of bread. She should've taken more care in her packing, but this temporary move had come on quickly. The day she decided to go to Island Park was the same day her friend Oriana had called to offer the cabin, rent already paid. Camille had protested, but Oriana's daughter was pregnant, and the doctors had discovered a serious birth defect. Oriana and her husband felt they needed to stay with her. Oriana had begged Camille on the other end of the line. "Please, Camille, use the cabin. I'd like to think something good came out of this."

"What do you mean?" she had asked with a stifled, confused voice.

"You need time away. You're on sabbatical to finish your book anyway. It'll be healing for you. Just think of this as your opportunity to become the person you've always wanted to be."

Then and there, she sealed her fate for the next two months.

"Mom?"

"Hmm?"

"Wouldn't the fact that witch covens always have thirteen people be another reason for the unluckiness of the number?"

Why didn't Darlene stop with these questions? "Maybe. Breakfast is ready."

After the prayer, they poured milk into gooey oats. Camille ate several bites before noticing her daughter studying a spoonful of steamy cereal. "What are you doing?"

"Looking at the black specs floating on top."

"What?"

"I swear there's a weevil lounging next to my oat."

Camille spat the cereal onto the table, pulling her bowl closer for inspection and finding brownish dots lying against several of her oats. Bolting up, she said, "Gross, they *are* weevils!" She dumped her bowl in the sink and gagged as she splashed a handful of water into her mouth.

Darlene burst into laughter.

"It's not funny!" Camille's protest was emphasized by the ringing of the phone.

Darlene picked up the phone, saying, "Ah, Mom, it's just protein. Hello," she said into the receiver, grabbing the pot. "Oh, my heck! There's thousands of them! Mom, didn't you notice?"

Camille stared blankly at her daughter. "I—I don't know. I must not have been looking."

"What? Oh, Mom made breakfast with weevils added for spice." Darlene peered into the cereal box. "Gross! They're crawling all over the place! How old is this cereal?"

Richard was on the other end, Camille realized, feeling like a deflating, worn-down, used tire.

"Sick!" Darlene shuddered. "They might crawl out of the box. What if they get into our other food?"

"Throw it away outside," Camille mumbled.

"Think it'll attract bears? I heard somewhere bears are attracted to any food left outside."

"I don't know," Camille said, slapping the table. "Which do you want? Weevils in your food or bears in the trash?"

"Mom!"

"Well?"

"The bears. I always wanted to see one in the open."

Camille grabbed the cereal box with the tips of her forefinger and thumb and rushed toward the door, leaving her daughter's excited chatting behind. She hustled toward the garage, the fresh wind gently brushing past her as she scanned the yard for Jackson. Nothing but trees, weeds, and clouds. He must have finished chopping the wood and gone home by now.

"Good," she said.

Halfway around the back, she paused and listened. Nothing. Where was nature's music? The rippling of water splashing onto the shore? The pleasant chirp of the birds? Maybe there was another squirrel lurking behind a tree waiting to attack. It had seen the success of its family member, enjoying the comforts of a freezing cabin, stocking up on crunchy weevils.

Her foot edged forward, cracking a twig. The sound echoed through the stillness as she scanned the horizon. Thick gray mist floated over the land, seeping between the trees. Were beady eyes peering from the fog? A tap echoed from far away, and she raced behind the garage. No trash cans. Where would they be? Distant noise broke the silence—definitely not the same sound as the hooting last night. She tripped over the cement step as she entered the garage and fell, scraping her chin. Oats and bugs spilled everywhere.

"Ugh," Camille said, glancing at the tiny black creatures. She stood, wiping her hands against her jeans, bumping the sliver in her finger. Wincing from the pain, she decided to pull the sliver out before doing anything else. "Halloween must have cast its spell," she mumbled.

"What are you talking about?"

Camille looked up to see the cold, hard, but attractive eyes of Jackson boring into her. She quickly glanced away, suddenly feeling hot.

"Nothing really." She continued her way to the house, losing most of her hobble. "Just about Halloween."

"What about it?" His words were sharp and hard.

She wondered what she had said wrong. "I regret getting out of bed this morning. Sometimes Halloween casts a spell of bad luck on people."

"Nonsense," Jackson said. "What's happened today that's so bad?"

That question shrunk Camille. It was as if he waved his magic wand, zapping her into a humiliated, reprimanded child who had been scolded for being hysterical over nothing.

"Forget I said anything. You would never understand."

"Try me."

"I don't think so," she said and continued to the cabin.

She made her way into the kitchen, limping with the pain. As she opened the refrigerator door, Darlene called from upstairs. "Mom, are you okay?" Camille wanted time to collect her dignity, but before she could collect anything at all, Darlene was at her side, insisting that she sit.

"What happened to your foot?" she asked after Camille slipped off her shoe.

Camille shrugged. To her relief, Darlene didn't press the issue, just made her a cold pack out of a washcloth and ice and pressed it on the injury.

"You need to be more careful. You're going to kill yourself. Richard's going to roast me if you hurt yourself any worse. You need a protective shield around you."

"Stop acting like Richard. Who's the mom anyway? Would you mind getting me the tweezers? I have a sliver." Darlene's eyebrows rose. "And would you sweep up the oat mess in the garage and pick up the logs by the front entry?"

"But Mom, weevils!"

"Thanks, dear, I don't know how I'd make it through this divorce without you," Camille said as Darlene's delicate mouth formed a pout. "And don't worry; there'll be no more incidents. Promise. We've had our share already."

"More incidents of what?"

Camille turned to see Jackson standing in the hall, arms loaded with wood. Her heart lurched. His eyes were no longer cold or hard but curious and warm. Flutters bounced around inside her stomach.

"Sorry," he said. "I knocked. I thought I heard someone say to come in. So what happened?"

"Oh, Mom's been having a lot of trouble today," Darlene said. "She—"

"That's quite enough, young lady," Camille jumped in before her daughter could say more. "Please hurry and get ready so we can go." Camille flicked a look at this man who kept showing up. She wondered how long he had been standing there.

Darlene left, and Jackson strolled around the scattered boxes, through the kitchen to the living room to fill the wood box. He eyed the empty fireplace with the logs drying on the hearth and then looked back to her foot propped on pillows. Her heart seemed to beat double-time as his eyes swept over her.

"Are you sure about doing the fire yourself?" he asked.

"Positive." No way would she give him the satisfaction of proving that she was incapable.

CHAPTER THREE

Jackson swung the ax, chopping rhythmically. He liked the sound and smell of splitting wood. Sweat dotted his forehead and neck, causing his hair to curl up above his collar. He paused from his labor to shed his coat and inhale the fresh air.

His muscles ached as he continued his chore, going over his plans for the day. Later he wanted to go into town to pick up supplies—not because he felt social, but because he needed food. He wished he didn't have to go shopping at all. He'd much rather blend into the scenery, leaving no distinction between him and the outdoors.

A dark fog seemed to seep inside him as he finished chopping the last of the logs and carried the wood to a stack by the swing. The swing, attached to a tree branch, hung motionless in the still morning. Would Camille or Darlene, or the other people staying with them use the swing during their stay, or would they be preoccupied by other things?

Until he moved here, he had been too busy with the daily grind. He'd never stopped for the simple things like swinging in dawn's light while listening to music. Now that he had been in Island Park for a while, he realized he had missed out. Instead of getting ahead of the game back in his so-called real life, he had depleted his soul. He was tempted to get on the swing himself after he finished stacking the wood, but if someone saw him, like the Britains, they might get annoyed. He had already bugged them enough for one day.

Not that he'd set out to annoy them. He paused, reviewing the facts. Camille had come outside to get logs for a fire. Sensing she was flustered, he did the gentlemanly thing and offered to carry in the wood. She'd turned him down flat and scurried away like a spooked squirrel. He waited what seemed an extraordinary amount of time for smoke to filter out the chimney. When that didn't happen, he made an excuse to go inside the cabin, planning on starting a fire without being noticed. Once inside, Darlene, the daughter, stared at him as if he had purple hair. What had he done?

He went over the scenario a couple more times and couldn't come up with a thing, except that Camille must be one of those beautiful, independent women who had "issues." He felt sorry for her husband, despite her very appealing eyes, and decided it'd be best to stay away as much as possible. The dark foggy feeling continued to settle in his chest.

The roar of a car caught his attention. He looked and nodded to Camille and Darlene as they drove past. Darlene waved. As he started to slip the hatchet into his belt loop, his hand stopped, fumbling awkwardly. His conversation with Camille had reminded him of superstition, of the bloated dead body, face down, in the mucky water. Pushing the thoughts away, he strode into the woods.

———

Most of the morning fog had lifted, but the grayish-blue clouds still lingered over the water. Withering grass bowed along the shoreline as the Britains' car bounced on the rutted road. "It's sad to see flowers dying," Darlene said as she thumbed through her plant and animal book.

"Um." Camille often associated the seasons with her own stages of life. Was she also browning as she headed into winter? She was young for winter, but sometimes that season sneaked up earlier than expected. As of late, she'd begun to sense that her life had already been lived. Was God forewarning her of an early death?

"Oh, stop the car, Mom. There's some flowers that still have blossoms."

Camille pulled to the side of the road, and clouds of dust settled on them when they climbed from the car. Wrinkling her nose, Darlene rushed to a translucent flower, sporting a dark purple-spotted center. "A sego lily, don't you think?" She glanced up, her long hair tumbling to one side.

Camille nodded and watched her daughter admire the shell-shaped flower. Both the flower and the daughter appeared fragile, but each was stronger than they seemed. The sego lily put up a good fight for life against approaching winter, and Darlene endured the divorce with grace. It was a crime that, with her strength and smarts, she refused to go to college, but in due time Camille would nudge her there.

A breeze tossed strands of Darlene's hair off her shoulders, a kiss from nature that made Camille smile. Maybe it would somehow protect Darlene and preserve her innocence even though it hadn't done the same for herself. Camille wondered how she was going to continue her life alone and on her own. Miserable. She'd wither away quietly like the flowers, unknown, her true self never fully bloomed. But her daughter could blossom.

Darlene checked off sego lily in her book and slid into the car. After securing her seatbelt, she returned to her book. Camille watched her. "You know, dear, you have a great love of learning. I don't see why you don't want to—"

"Mom, I'm not going to college."

"You're always reading and asking questions. What do you have against it?"

"The structure. I like to study what I want when I want."

"But your education will have holes and gaps. You won't know what you—"

"I don't have to live life like you and Dad. I am an autodidactic person."

This silenced Camille. She hated being accused of being anything like Adam, and to have it come from her own daughter made it that much worse.

When they arrived at the island's entrance, she fumbled around the dashboard for the card to open the electric gate. A hardy-looking elderly lady, dressed in a flannel coat, jeans, and brown boots, marched up to them. Camille rolled down her window.

"I'm Phyllis Westguard," the woman said. "My husband and I watch over the island." Her face was covered with soft wrinkles, and her high cheeks, defined bone structure, and crystal blue eyes made her striking.

"Nice to meet you." Camille extended her hand.

"Hope you're looking for solitude because we're approaching the quiet season. The birds and most people have gone south, and the animals around here are hibernating."

"We heard an owl last night," Darlene said.

"There are a few of those around, and woodpeckers."

Camille remembered the knocking sound earlier and was thinking about mentioning it when Phyllis asked, "Have you met Jackson yet?"

"Yeah, we met him last—" Camille's sentence was interrupted by an elderly man who seemed to come out of nowhere.

He extended his arthritic hand. "Bryce Westguard." He had friendly wrinkles piled onto each other and was thin as the twig he twirled in his worn hands.

They shook hands as Phyllis rambled on. "She was going to tell me if she's met Jackson yet." Bryce nodded. Phyllis's eyes held a spark as she waited.

A busybody, Camille thought as she looked into the woman's face. Still, she knew she had to answer them so she said, "Yeah, last night."

"Isn't he wonderful?" Phyllis responded. "He's led the most interesting life."

Growing increasingly uncomfortable hearing about a man she'd rather forget, Camille changed the subject. "Do you know the best way of getting a squirrel out of the cabin?"

The couple laughed. "Those darn critters are devils to get rid of," Phyllis said. "There's only one way. It might sound odd, but it works. You get a quart jar and lay it against the floorboard, and the squirrel will run into it. It won't see the glass, you see. Squirrels always stick close to the wall, and they go real fast when you chase them. They'll plow right into the jar. You'll need to catch the varmint before it starves. Them squirrels sure smell after they've been dead a while."

"Thanks for the advice," Camille said.

"You're welcome." Phyllis patted the window frame, giving a wave as they took off.

"I'm sure the Native Americans didn't use mason jars," Darlene said.

"The Native Americans didn't live in cabins or have heaters," Camille said.

It wasn't long before the car hit the deep ruts in the dirt parking lot of the gas station. They parked next to a beat-up white truck where several kids wiggled in the back of the bed, playing with their father's rusty tools. Camille nodded as she passed them. One of the boys flicked something onto the ground. "Don't, Johnny," the other boy whined. "You'll get us in trouble." A couple who looked like the older version of the kids walked out of the store, holding hands. As Camille approached, the husband gazed into his wife's eyes, smiling before he kissed her.

Camille brushed by them, going straight into the store. Darlene soon joined her with Bisquick, milk, and eggs. They made it to the counter, where an old man with wrinkles as pronounced as Ripple's potato chips smiled at them. The man keyed their items in the register and said, "A storm's comin'. It's a shame it's going to rain on your barbecue."

"Just heating our cabin," Camille said.

"Uh, you weren't planning on starting a fire in the house with lighter fluid, were you?" he asked. "You'll blow yourself up. If you don't know about fires, you should have your husband make a fire before you kill yourself . . . Look, lady, if you need help, how about hiring Jackson Armstrong? He's been getting quite the repetition around here for doing that kind of thing."

"How much do I owe you?" she asked, paid him, and then marched out grumbling.

She drove in silence until Darlene said, "Uh, Mom, the front tire's sinking."

"What?" She pulled the car off the side of the road to find a nail sticking out of the treads. "Let's see if we can make it home before it goes flat."

"Mom, that'd ruin the rim of your tire."

"Great." Camille plopped down on a log, the cool wind chilling her face. Darlene leaned against the hood of the car and didn't say a word. Ten minutes passed with nothing said until a billowing cloud of dust hovered in the distance.

"Think it's coming this way?" Camille asked, slightly rocking the log beneath her.

Her daughter shrugged but remained quiet while an orange, beat-up hillbilly truck approached. It didn't show signs of slowing.

All at once, an animal darted out of the hollow log. The small creature was covered with thick black fur and sported a white stripe down its head, which continued along its body, breaking off in two different lines on its tail. Camille screamed.

The skunk stomped.

"It's going to squirt me!" she squeaked, her voice high and terrified. She longed to run, but only her mouth worked while the rest of her body refused to budge. It raised itself on its front legs. Its tail rose. Her pulse pounded in her ear. She was going to get it. She was going to get . . . The animal turned, and a long spray of yellow liquid nailed her sweater. The most malodorous smell filled her lungs, taking her breath. She screamed and fell off the log, and the striped animal scurried off.

"Aaaua!" Camille threw off her sweater. Tears streamed down her face as she approached the truck that had pulled up about two feet away.

A man wearing a denim shirt leaned over to the passenger side of his truck and rolled down the window. "Are you okay?" His nose twitched at the undeniable skunk odor that filled the once-aromatic woods.

Just her luck, it was Jackson. Could her day get any worse?

Camille looked in disgust in the direction the skunk had vanished. "At first, I thought it was a black cat," she said with a hiccup. She was coming close to a scream as she held her nose. "Oh, that stupid creature!"

Darlene walked away from Camille, laughing behind her hand.

"It's not funny!" Camille protested, holding back a sob. "I could smell like this for weeks."

"You need help?" Jackson asked.

"I was sprayed by a skunk!"

"I can tell."

"Thanks a lot," Camille said.

"I mean no offense, but you don't smell like a petunia."

"What am I supposed to do?" Even to her own ears, she sounded hysterical. And she couldn't stop her heart from beating faster. That wasn't because Jackson was there. It wasn't! She wasn't in the least attracted to him, no matter how ruggedly good looking he was.

"Get rid of your sweater. You'll probably stink for days."

"What!"

"Could be longer. It's hard to say."

"First, my tire goes flat, and now I smell like a sewer!"

He shifted his truck into park. "It'll be all right. I got a tidbit that might make you feel better. Some people use the foul-smelling liquid of skunk for perfume."

"It's not funny."

"I wasn't joking. Do you want help with your tire?"

"No, that's . . . yeah, I guess so."

"Do you or don't you? I don't want to press."

"She does," Darlene said.

Jackson nodded at Darlene but waited for Camille's consent. "If you don't want me helping, it's fine. Here, let me lend you my cell phone. You can call your husband." The man dug in his back pocket and pulled out his phone. Camille stared at him. He waved the phone in front of her. "Take it."

"Keep it. I don't need it," she said flatly.

"Course you do. If you haven't noticed, you're stranded by the roadside, and a storm's approaching. And you don't seem to be the most handy person."

She peered at the horizon to see dark clouds rolling toward them.

"Come on."

She looked at his rough whiskers, at Darlene, then to the car. Finally, she had no choice to admit, "I have no one to call. I'm not married."

"I don't care about your personal life," Jackson said gruffly. "Call the people you're staying with." He swung the phone in front of her again.

She stood there without replying, her heart thudding painfully against her chest. She let her gaze wander away from the windowsill and over the equipment on the bed of his truck.

"You came up to this country by yourself?" He sounded incredulous.

"What if I did?" She held out her chin squarely.

"Ah, nothing. Come on; I'll teach you how to change a tire."

"Thanks." She took a step away from the door to allow him to exit.

"This isn't any of my business," Jackson said as they walked to the car, "but you shouldn't have come out here without learning a few basic survival skills."

"No lectures," Camille said, her jaw clenching.

Jackson stopped and gazed down at her. "I'm just trying to help." He lifted his hat and ran his hand through his unkempt hair.

Camille wrinkled her nose. Why had she ever thought this man attractive? He stunk almost as bad as she did.

"Pardon my appearance. I've been working on my truck. It—has an oil leak. Ain't leakin' no more."

"Isn't," Camille corrected instinctively.

"No lectures," he said.

29

"One should always use correct grammar. How we speak reflects who we are."

"Spoken like a true educated snob." Jackson strode ahead of her in complete confidence, as though he hadn't just launched a verbal bomb.

Adam had often played warfare like that. Brutal attacks, then complete innocence, staring in shock that she was upset. He would deny ever saying anything, much less something so mean. "What do you take me for anyway?" he'd asked once. "A heartless brute?" The memories, the layers of years of hurt from swallowing the attacks raged in Camille. No more would she tolerate the name-calling, the picking, the pecking at her identity.

"You can leave now," she roared at Jackson. "I don't need your help after all."

"Sure thing, lady. You're the one that'll be stuck in the storm. Do you want to hop into the bed of my truck?"

"No."

"You don't have a choice. Either get in or you'll be stuck in this storm, and believe me, it won't be pretty."

"We'll be fine."

"Mom!" Darlene cried.

"Very well then." He took off in his truck down the road, leaving them in a cloud of dust.

Her daughter turned to her and screeched, "How could you do that?"

"You wouldn't understand." She breathed deeply, trying to calm herself. "It'd be stupid to put ourselves at his mercy. There are too many rapes and murders today for us to take chances."

"You could've at least let him fix our tire. Now what are we going to do?"

"Walk."

A few sprinkles fell on their heads. "But the storm," Darlene said.

"We'll have to be pioneers or Indians and just plow through it. Let's get our groceries and go."

Her sweater had fallen close to the car, and the smell made

Camille's stomach want to revolt. She remembered her weevil-infested oatmeal and slammed the door shut, turning in time to see a black feral cat crawl out of the forest. Of all the days to run into a black cat! With the skunk she'd lost every bit of reserved strength, and now she was freezing and smelly.

"It's okay. It's okay," she said to herself. The cat approached, his green eyes staring through her. "I know, I know," Camille said. "You're a British black cat?"

"Why British?" Darlene was rounding the back of the car, but she stopped when she spotted the cat.

"Because to the British, a black cat represents good luck."

A loud ripple of thunder echoed across the mountain range. The sprinkles grew into quarter-size drops. "American cat, I tell you," Camille said, stifling a sob. "And on Halloween too."

Camille wondered what more problems crossing the path of a black cat on Halloween might bring. What else could possibly go wrong?

CHAPTER FOUR

That long-ago day had been hot, sultry, and thick with mirage from the blazing sun. On those type of days there was only one thing for a teenage boy in Colorado to do, and that was to dive deep into the dark canal, emerging revitalized. Only one problem stood in Jackson's way: his mother. He was sixteen, almost a man, and his mom thought she had control over him, his life, and everything he did. Her fear of misfortune had grasped hold of the family, choking them like a madman, squeezing out the last air bubbles of life. Three years previously, his dad could handle it no longer and gasped for air by leaving her and his two sons.

His father's desertion only made his mother more controlling and more caught up in her paranoid belief that fate waited to pounce on her and her family. Swimming in the canal was too risky—at least, that was the way his mom looked at it. That was why Jackson and his brother, Billy, were sneaking out of the house to do what every other kid on the block did with their parents' blessing.

"Where do you two think you're going?" his mom had asked when she caught them at the side door. Her jaw clenched, making her chin look sharper than normal.

"Swimmin'."

"No."

Jackson, not being one to be discouraged easily and knowing the power of his charm, said, "Don't worry, Ma." He pressed a kiss to her cheek and playfully snapped his beach towel at her legs. But this time his mom would have no fooling; instead she clasped onto his shoulder and said, "It's Friday the Thirteenth. No good comes with tempting fate. Don't do it, Jackson. Don't sneak behind my back, thinking you're pulling the wool over my eyes. You don't want to be responsible for what could happen."

"Ma, no one believes in that stuff, 'cept you."

"It doesn't mean it's not true."

He grew angry. "You're too uptight about things. Always worrying, smothering us with your fears." It had been a mean thing to say. His father had often said that behind closed doors, especially toward the end of their marriage, late at night when his parents thought he and his brother slept.

His mother slapped Jackson, then stormed out to the backyard. Jackson turned to his brother and tried to laugh the scene off. "Let's go," he said.

"Buuuut, what about Mom?" Billy's face flushed. He liked to coddle their mother.

Their mom hadn't been the only one hurt by their dad's departure, and Jackson wouldn't play the "protect Mommy and do whatever she says because she's been hurt enough" game. "Are you a cluck-cluck-cluck?" He flapped his arms like they were wings.

"I'm no chicken. It's just that—"

"You know you can't beat me," Jackson sneered. "That's why you're chickening out."

"Shut up," Billy snapped.

Jackson could tell he had gotten to him, but he had to act fast before his brother thought out the situation more clearly. He grabbed the towel he'd dropped on the floor and snapped it at Billy with the same flare he had used on their mother. "Too bad you lost your chance to jumpstart on the race," he said, taking off to the canal. He heard Billy behind him. Jackson glanced around and could tell he had aggravated his little brother from the way he tore after him. This race had promise, and Jackson knew he'd have to give it his all to maintain his bragging rights. It wasn't long before both boys treaded through the brown, cool, bug-filled water, trying to beat each other across.

———

Camille's refusal to ride back to the cabin with Jackson struck a nerve. It was almost as if she knew his crime and judged him to be no good. Not the type she would ride with even if she were stranded miles away from her cabin with her daughter and the reality of a mean storm on its way.

The light sprinkles of rain he had left her standing in had increased to a downpour. He switched the windshield wipers on and then hit the steering wheel with the palm of his hand. "Damn that woman," he said aloud. He flipped on the radio and searched for a station, but the storm distorted the frequency. He snapped off the radio.

Should he turn around? The ruts in the road made up his mind for him. He was in a rut all right. Every time he tried to do anything nice where a female was concerned, he fell in deeper. Better to avoid them. Besides, women brought pain much worse than the jolts from the potholes. A picture of his ex-wife's beautifully deceptive face, with her china doll features, flashed into his mind. Why did she leave him? He remembered the sick feeling in his gut so vividly as he had begged her once more to explain as she exited their door for the last time.

She had released her grip on the knob, glanced at him, then cast her emerald gaze to the floor. In a low, strained tone, she asked, "Do you really want to know?" He had nodded. "Fine, I'll tell you. Jaxy, you would never dream of not using American cheese on your noodles. It's like you haven't heard of Swiss cheese."

"Cheese? What does cheese have to do with it?"

"You're so predictable. You look at a bag of chips and try to decide the best way to open it to avoid a spill. I want someone spontaneous enough to rip it open from the bottom without thinking."

"Give me a chance."

"It wouldn't be natural for you. I don't know what I thought I'd be getting when I entered this relationship." She shook her head, causing her blond hair to bounce. He longed to run his hands through the silky locks, pull her close, and make her his. Maybe it would—

"It's not only that," she added. "It's the way you try to rule me. You made me have a child when you knew I didn't want one."

How could she accuse him of that? "But . . . I thought . . . you love him."

"You don't meet my emotional needs, either—always pulling away, running into the cave, or whatever the psychologists call it now." Maggie tugged her purse strap back onto her shoulder. "I'm sorry, but this is for the best. I stayed until Austin was old enough. My jail term's up." She kissed his cheek and left. He'd heard nothing from her since —three long months.

Jackson had heard a psychologist on the radio explaining that breaking up was harder on men than women because men needed closure. They longed to understand why relationships turned sour, and if they couldn't logically explain it, they became obsessive. The doc was absolutely right. If only he could switch off his thoughts, his well-organized and logical arguments as to why she was wrong and why she should've stayed, and how he was the hopeless victim.

Now another woman flooded his thoughts: Camille Britain. She seemed so helpless—a damsel in distress. He longed, despite his better judgment, to be Sir Galahad and slip on a knight's shining armor to rescue her and her daughter. But she, like all the other modern women he'd run into, wouldn't let him. What had happened to the good old days when a man knew his role—to be a gentleman, protector, provider—and a woman would be flattered? He gazed into the midst of the angry thunderclouds. Camille would pay a heavy price for insisting to walk.

The thought gave him no satisfaction.

———

Two hours passed while they walked in the howling wind and winter-scented air. Finally, the dull gray gate came into view. "The gate," Camille said, exhausted.

"I hope this will teach you, Mom. When a nice, good-looking man tries to help you—let him."

Camille lifted her chin into the wind, ignoring her daughter. Muddy water splashed over her slip-on shoes, seeping through to her socks, the icy cold water soothing her foot that was now even more swollen than it had been after the accident in the garage. She glanced at her daughter's white, glistening skin, which held a trace of goose bumps. Thick strands of wet, black hair stuck artistically onto her face, as if a painter had painstakingly placed each strand into its proper place. She wore a royal blue windbreaker, which she'd zipped to the last tooth, and her cherry red nose stuck halfway under the fabric. No wonder boys tripped over themselves to impress her. How would she stop her daughter from falling for the wrong guy like she'd done?

"Is that the security guard?"

Startled, Camille looked up to where her daughter pointed. A cozy pine cabin sat along the side of the gate with a dark shadow in front. "Either it's a person or a tree."

"I hope it's the security guard and that she'll give us a ride the rest of the way home. Your bad luck spell has to end," Darlene said. She brushed at the hair stuck to her face, ruining the painting but instantly replacing it with another masterpiece.

"Seeing a black cat makes me doubt there'll be an end."

"You're so negative," Darlene said.

The comment cut through Camille like a jagged knife. How many times had she heard Adam complain of the same thing? "That's enough," Camille said.

"It's true."

An awkward silence stretched between them as they came upon the metal gate. The distant object they hoped would be the security guard turned out to be a decaying tractor.

"Did you remember to bring the key to the gate?" Darlene asked.

The key. It was back in the car on the side of the road, miles away. She had remembered to grab the key to the cabin, but the one to the gate had been on a separate ring. "We'll have to climb."

It wasn't until Camille was almost over the gate that a jolting pain shot through her back, causing her body to stiffen. She fell, dazed.

"Mom! Are you okay?" Darlene sounded panicked.

"Yeah. I think so," Camille managed, but she didn't actually think she could stand up.

"I'll get help. Nope!" Darlene held up a finger. "Don't even tell me no."

"I was just going to say to hurry," Camille lied.

Darlene flagged down the next person who passed and had the man carry Camille to the Westguards' cabin for immediate medical attention. As the man carried Camille, he commented that she looked like a frozen Popsicle. *A humiliated Popsicle,* Camille thought when the story of the skunk and the flat tire came out.

The Westguards existed quite well without a car, apparently, so a ride home wasn't possible, but they did know what would help with the stink—betadine. They also gave her a lecture on what a peaceful animal a skunk was—how they only squirted at danger and that they lifted their tail or stomped their feet in warning before that. Camille was too achy and cold to care much about anything, but Mrs. Westguard must have thought Camille was uncomfortable because she said, "You do know that people make perfume out of the skunk's liquid." Camille groaned as she thought back to Jackson and the effort he had made earlier to cheer her up. She'd have to apologize.

After Camille took care of her smell as much as she could and caught her breath, she decided she'd imposed on the Westguards enough, though the wind still howled and the cozy cabin creaked under its blast. Camille forced her chilled-to-the-bone limbs to move, trudging through the weather. The rain had finally lessened to a light sprinkle and then stopped as they approached the cabin, the heavy gray cloud cover lifting its shroud off the ground and revealing a golden glow of a sun that already hung low in the sky. The peaceful view made Camille feel slightly better despite the day, which had been almost entirely wasted.

Once inside the cabin, her peace was ruined. Moving boxes waited to be emptied, and clutter was scattered throughout the small cabin, but the most upsetting sight was a pile of bread crumbs on the dining room table that could have only been made by their unwelcome guest, the squirrel. "Darlene, would you please put the Mason jar in the corner and see if that'll really work?"

Darlene did so without comment, for which Camille was grateful.

When a sudden movement caught her attention, Camille looked up toward her daughter and saw a tail disappearing around the corner of the kitchen wall. "Quick! Guard that side of the room so I can drive him head-on into the bottle."

The squirrel stayed along the wall. After ten minutes of maneuvering, they chased him into the bottle, the squirrel screaming in high-pitched wails.

"I'm not taking that jar out," Darlene yelled. "No way."

That left Camille with no choice. She squared her shoulders and said, "I'll do it."

"What if it bites?" Darlene asked. "What if it is a carrier of all sorts of germs? What if you get some deadly disease and die because he bit you? What if—"

Camille closed her eyes. Holding firmly to the wiggling jar, she hurried outside and tipped the Mason bottle, causing one foot to dangle out, then another foot, and at last a head. The creature scurried away.

"Way to go, Mom! You scared it half to death. He won't be dumb enough to mess with you again."

With a smile, Camille patted her daughter on the shoulder. "Since I got the creature, you get to do the sterilizing."

The way Darlene's nose wrinkled in disgust was much like Adam's expression when he was frustrated. Camille couldn't shake that image as she filled the tub with hot water. *I won't worry about that,* she thought, pushing it from her mind.

It wasn't long before iridescent bubbles floated through the small bathtub. She rested her head against the rim of the tub and closed her eyes, refusing to think of anything but the water on her aching body. When the water cooled, she let some out and filled it up with hot water again, not wanting to leave the room that had become her sanctuary from a really rotten day. She'd just started dozing when her peace was interrupted by a loud crashing sound. Hurried footsteps moved across the cabin toward the front. "Mom! There's a truck wrapped around that tree out back by the road. You better come see."

Quickly, Camille wrapped herself in a bathrobe and met the onslaught of Darlene and her questions as they hustled outside. "Do you think anyone's alive? Mom, aren't you going to see if anyone needs help?"

A boom echoed through the trees. Both she and Darlene screamed as a large man with cowboy boots and hat came around the hood of the truck to stand in the early afternoon shadow. "Is everyone all right?" Camille called to the figure, whose features were obscured in the darkness.

"All but Sam."

"Should I call an ambulance?"

"An ambulance wouldn't help." He took a step away from the truck.

Someone had died. Tears sprang to her eyes, and she rubbed her hands over them as he came closer.

"Oh, lady, don't cry. I'll just get Sam to a mechanic."

"A mechanic?" Her voice wavered as she looked up into Jackson's familiar face.

"Yeah, aren't they the people to call when your car's sick?"

Camille was all too aware of Jackson's eyes looking at her face and falling down over her robe. Her hair was probably stingy and her makeup smeared—had she even put any on this morning? And why did she care how she looked around him anyway? Especially after the fight they'd had earlier.

"Sam's your truck?" Darlene asked.

"Yep." He glanced at Camille, who clutched her robe more tightly around her. "Who did you think he was, my grandpa?"

Avoiding his gaze, Camille nodded at the truck, hoping it was dark enough that he couldn't see the flush on her face. "That's a nasty crash. I bet your wife's going to kill you. Definitely earned yourself the couch, if not the porch."

The man's brown eyes stared into Camille's, unwavering for what seemed an eternity. "I don't have a wife anymore."

"Oh," Camille said, feeling rather like an idiot.

He still stared.

Was her robe too sheer or something? She was positive the terrycloth wasn't see-through, but maybe the light from the back porch behind her made it so anyway. She stepped further to the side. "Wh—what happened?"

Jackson blinked, his stare intensifying. "She left me nine months ago. I'm not sure why. I guess I'm not the easiest person to live with." He gave a chuckle that sounded more like a grunt.

"No," Camille said, sensing her red face transforming to a deep crimson. "I'm sorry. I wouldn't dream of asking something so personal. I meant, what happened to Sam."

"Sam?"

"Your truck." She motioned toward the twisted metal.

"Oh, that. You see, I was driving along and a big moose darted in front of me. I swerved to miss her. Before I knew it, my truck introduced itself to your tree."

"A moose?" Darlene asked.

"She's here all the time. Sometimes she and her calf pass your place to get a drink."

Darlene peered in the night. "She has a calf?"

"Yeah, but I haven't seen the calf for a while, so maybe it's moved on." He rubbed his chin. "Actually, I haven't seen the moose around much either. I thought they'd migrate by now. Sure took me by surprise."

"Did you miss it?" Darlene asked.

"I wasn't even close. Wish I could say the same for the tree." He walked toward the broken trunk and rubbed the stubble on his chin again. "That tree'll probably die."

"At least it's not an oak," Camille said.

"Why?" Darlene asked.

"There's a legend that a man cut an oak down after he broke his leg. From then on the others who witnessed the fallen tree experienced bad luck. Of course, oaks don't grow in this part of the country. But right after you wrecked, I heard a loud, woeful sound, almost like a cry. In the book—oh, what was it published in . . . I think *Natural History of Wiltshire,* it says something like: 'when an oak is feeling, it gives a kind of shriek or groan that may be heard a mile off, as if it were the genius of the oak lamenting.' When I saw the tree and remembered the sound I heard, I naturally thought of an oak."

Jackson laughed. "That's the weirdest thing I ever heard."

Camille fingered her robe again. She was babbling about superstition. She needed to stop it. Not only was it a bad habit, but it probably came off as crazy to Jackson.

"Interesting attire." His eyes ran down the robe again.

"Thank you for noticing," she said. She couldn't help seeing that his deep brown eyes were set close to his nose, a sign of someone with an Evil Eye, which gave a person the ability to cast spells without even knowing it. Myths had it that they could bring bad luck to humans and animals alike, and their power even extended to destroying inanimate objects.

Of course, she really didn't believe in that nonsense. She *wouldn't!* And to prove it, she wouldn't let herself cross her fingers to ward off the effects of the Evil Eye.

Meanwhile, Jackson was still staring at her. She felt undressed—which, in a way, she kind of was. His eyes sure were compelling, if a woman liked the rough, outdoors type. Ugh. It was definitely time to end the chitchat. "Glad nobody but *Sam* was hurt," she said. "I guess we'll see you again sometime."

"Hey, wait a minute. I need help getting my truck off this tree," Jackson said.

"That's a problem."

"Could you give me a pull?"

"My car's not strong enough."

"I bet it is," he said. "Your car has four-wheel drive." His teasing grin reminded her of a young boy, but the rest of his features, from the whiskers to the firm, determined jaw, spoke of manliness. There was something irresistible about the mixture of boy and man.

"My car still has a flat tire," she said. "It's still back on the road somewhere. I—I shouldn't have yelled at you earlier. I'm sorry."

"Apology accepted, but you do need to learn some basic skills."

She turned her back on him and headed toward her cabin.

"Wait a minute."

She faced him. "Why?"

"I'm sorry. I'll fix your tire if you'll pull me away from this tree."

"I'm not walking back to my car to get it."

"Give me the key, and I'll go myself."

"Why should I trust you?" Camille asked. Darlene cleared her throat and tugged on Camille's robe to show her displeasure, but Camille didn't care. Her daughter knew nothing about men.

Jackson looked at Camille, and her heartbeat increased percep-tively as she gazed back. "If you want your car fixed, now's the chance," he said. "You don't know how to change a tire, and I doubt if you'll be able to find anyone else to help since most people have left for the winter. Of course, you might get lucky on Thanksgiving."

"All right, all right. I'll get the key." She made her way through the weeds, shivering. Another cold breeze had settled on the land. She noted that her daughter stayed behind with Jackson. "Darlene, come here a minute."

"What, Mom?" Darlene asked when she got close.

Camille whispered, her gaze flicking to Jackson and back again, "I don't want you alone with him."

"He seems fine to me."

"Trust me."

"But—"

"Trust," Camille said in her it-is-settled voice. They walked to the door, and Camille turned the handle. It didn't budge. She tried it again. Still, the door wouldn't open.

"Is it locked?" Darlene asked.

"Yes."

"Why would—?"

Camille sighed. "I locked it after we came home. I was positive we'd have no reason to go anywhere for the rest of the day."

"I'll get Jackson." Darlene glanced back to where Jackson still waited for the key. He appeared to be examining the damage to his truck.

"Don't." Camille clutched the sleeve of her daughter's shirt.

"Why?"

"We can figure it out ourselves. I don't want my more comments about me not knowing how to survive. I'm a history professor for heaven sakes! The least I can do is figure out how to get into my own cabin." With that she headed around the stack of logs. "I'm going to check the front door. Why don't you try the windows?"

"Mom, this is silly."

Camille rushed to the front porch, listening to the water of the lake hit the shoreline with an insistent rustle. Her bathrobe flapped open, exposing her calf with each step. She paid no heed and focused on the locked brass door. She tried to open it again, pulling harder. A few cuss words escaped her mouth. "Oh, please," she muttered. If he found out, Jackson would get that proud laughing look with his eyebrows raised, though why she cared about that she didn't know. She was being as silly as a schoolgirl.

Camille returned to the back where Darlene waited, apparently also having had no luck. "Can I get Jackson now?" Darlene asked.

Camille pursed her lips. "That's not an option."

"Why not?" Both Darlene and Camille peered up in surprise to see Jackson watching them with raised eyebrows. The hot burner on Camille's face flared. She grabbed the cord that wrapped around her bathrobe to make sure it was secure.

"What do you need help with?" he asked.

"We're locked out of our house," Darlene said with a smile.

Camille felt her stomach drop. Her daughter was using her best damsel-in-distress ploy. Jackson flashed his deep brown eyes on Camille, but she forced herself to look at a distant tree. "I know—this stupid woman shouldn't be in the wilderness. Can't even get into her own cabin."

"I wanted to know if you had a screwdriver handy. I've given you enough credit to have already tried the windows. That is, if you don't mind me helping?" Jackson asked, continuing to watch her.

She flinched. "Doesn't seem like I have much of a choice unless I want to spend a cold night in the woods in my bathrobe."

He strolled to the garage with his head tilted back. Darlene fell into step behind him while Camille trudged after both of them. Maybe she could redeem herself by reading the Boy Scout Handbook tonight and changing her own tire. But what was she thinking? She didn't *want* to change her tire. And who cared what Jackson thought?

When they had all stepped into the garage, Camille said, "The screwdriver is on the top shelf."

"I see you managed to snoop around in the garage already. You've had a full day," Jackson said with an amused smile.

Darlene laughed. "Mom always has lots of things happen on Halloween and also on Friday the Thirteenth. You see—"

"Darlene!" Camille scowled at her.

The girl giggled. "My mom's extremely superstitious. She's made a study about it and is writing a book. She's trying to prove that superstition is based on fact."

Jackson glanced at Camille.

"The book is not on superstition. It's on Yellowstone wildflowers," she said.

"Ever believe in having a bad day?" He grabbed the screwdriver.

"There's been too many things happening today and every Halloween," Darlene said.

"Then why am I not having a—"

"Your truck," Darlene answered with a grin.

"I don't believe in superstition," Jackson snapped. Camille and Darlene stared at him. "But that's the only bad thing. After all, I did get to see you two again." He smiled.

"Not everyone gets inundated with bad luck on Halloween," Camille said.

"Why would the fates pick you?" His glance held a sudden tenderness. "You seem like a harmless person."

"I don't know why some people are picked and others aren't. Maybe certain types of people are more susceptible," Camille said.

He shrugged. "Maybe it happens more to people who dwell on it."

She decided to ignore that and took the lead back to the cabin, continuing the sermon. "A lot of the medieval people turned to superstition. They lived in constant fear with plagues or starvation knocking daily at their door. They needed certain rules or a system to live by. It gave the people a sense of control."

As Jackson worked on opening one of the front windows, he said, "Superstition is just a placebo."

"I don't use anything as a placebo." Her voice shook when she said this. Her anger slipped out into her tone, but she also recognized the vulnerability, the hurt. If Jackson were a female, he would have picked up on that instantly, but chances were good he would be clueless and continue on with their bantering. But just to be safe, she watched him for clues. His broad back bent over, his muscles shifting under his shirt as he worked the window. Camille couldn't help noticing how muscular and healthy looking he was. Adam and a lot of their acquaintances, both men and women, had given up on fitness decades ago.

Not only did Jackson not go on with the conversation, but he didn't speak at all until the window was open and Darlene climbed inside.

Then Jackson stood and faced Camille, his brown eyes peering straight into hers. She met his gaze, refusing to turn from his stare, though she desperately wanted to. A feeling of concern seemed to flow from him to her. This was too much. She looked away.

"I wasn't talking about you." His voice reflected the concern his presence communicated. "I mean, I don't think you use superstition as a placebo."

What should she say to that? Because maybe she did—a little.

"Welcome home!" Darlene exclaimed as she threw open the front door, her arms spread out wide.

Jackson stepped back to allow Camille to go through first. She walked in, scooting boxes out of the way. Jackson strolled behind her, going straight into the living room. "You've got a leak," he said, his breath forming a puff of a cloud as he spoke. "And why isn't your heat working?"

"We've been freezing since we got here," Darlene said.

Camille shot her daughter a look. "That is enough."

"What?" Darlene asked with an exaggerated shrug.

Jackson's deep voice interrupted this mother-daughter interaction. "Did you light the pilot?"

"The what?" Both Camille and Darlene asked.

"The wick on the heater. The cabin runs on propane."

"Doesn't sound too hard to fix," Camille said.

"Tell you what." Jackson turned and stepped close to Camille. His swift movement intensified Camille's awareness of him. He took command of the room just by his presence. He rubbed his hands together, making a scratchy sound, and she watched the rough, weathered hands. "I'll fix your tire, get the heat pumping nice and warm, *and* repair the leak in the roof, if you'll give me a ride to Yellowstone tomorrow."

"I don't—"

"Just for the day. Take me in the morning and we'll return in the evening. I wouldn't ask, but I really have to shoot bears."

"What?" Darlene shrieked.

"Shoot, as in photographs for a magazine. I've got a deadline, and my editor will kill me if I don't get them."

"I—I don't know."

"She means yes," Darlene said. Camille glared. "Mom, I'm sick of freezing. How else are we going to get warm?"

"We'd be leaving early in the morning," Jackson said. "Before the . . ."

But Camille didn't hear the rest of Jackson's instructions because of the buzz of the phone. She dove over several boxes, grasping for the receiver. "Hello?" she panted.

"Mom. I've been trying to call you for hours," Richard said. "How was your day?"

Camille could hear a faint crying in the background. "I don't want to talk about it."

Despite her son's continued demands, Camille didn't give in. No way was she going to relive that day or make herself appear a victim. Finally Richard gave up trying to pull information out of her. "Don't tell me then, but I do know one thing, and that is your bad luck must've worn off onto your grandson. He's had nothing but accidents today." The crying grew louder. "There he goes again."

"Is he okay?" Camille asked.

After a delay, Richard said, "Yeah, but I better go. You'd think since my mother's in a different state I could escape this, but no. She had to send her bad luck down a generation to her grandson."

"I had nothing to do with—"

"I know. I've just had a long day. I'm glad to hear Halloween didn't kill you even though you won't tell me what happened."

"Darlene's not going to tell either."

"Fine." Richard said goodbye. Camille turned to find Jackson waiting for her answer.

"Okay," she said to Jackson. "You have a deal."

CHAPTER FIVE

The sun set low in the sky as Jackson jogged to the crunched truck and opened the undamaged door. It creaked in protest. He reached for the flashlight under the front seat. He'd have to hurry if he wanted to make it to Camille's car before the daylight vanished. Once on the dirt road, his pace increased to a trot, and he began reflecting on the day. Wrapping his truck around a tree like a smashed pop can ranked high on his list of the stupidest thing he had ever done. He wouldn't have felt so foolish if he hadn't been listening to his messages on his cell phone. Ironic that the voice of his ex-wife and the sight of a moose occurred at the same time.

Maggie wouldn't have called for no reason. She must be after something, but what? All she said on the message was, "Hey Jaxy, give me a call." Then she left a number, which he traced to Los Angeles. What she was doing there was a mystery, but so were most of the other things she did. Her voice had been so airy, so carefree. Not the voice of someone who had divorced him. No depression, bitterness, anger, or any of that stuff. Just like they were happy as ever and she wanted to tell him of the newest friend she had made.

He rubbed the keys Camille had given him, and thoughts of her ran through his mind—a welcome change from thinking about

Maggie. Camille was anything but practical. She'd screamed at seeing a black cat, rambled on about not hurting an oak, and then explained why the medieval people had created such silliness. Definitely passionate and too emotional. But she did look cute with her hazel eyes enlarging as she spoke, her hair wet and uncombed. The robe had been completely modest, but it didn't hide enough of that great figure. Or maybe he just had an overactive imagination. He kicked a rock from under his cowboy boots into the shrubs.

Camille's looks were more rustic than his ex-wife's. Her sporty brown hair reached her shoulders, and her facial features were an average size instead of the daintiness that marked Maggie's. In fact, if anything, Maggie was too thin. Her defined nose turned slightly upward at the tip, and she had fragile cheekbones that stood out in her narrow face. He'd always thought of Maggie as an expensive china dish with integral artwork. By contrast, Camille was a simple tailored plate—strong, too, like steel that wouldn't break or given in. Maggie's interests varied depending on her mood. Camille seemed focused on a subject and on learning it thoroughly. When it came to family, Maggie had little time, but Camille brought her daughter on her vacation. The women were so different that it was like comparing the mountains to the sea.

He stopped his thoughts short. What was he thinking? Maggie was gone from his life, and he wasn't involved with Camille—or about to get involved. He'd fled to Island Park to discover nature, not to find another woman. He'd had a few exchanges with Camille, that was all, and he mostly seemed to annoy her.

That's okay. I'm not interested in her, either. But Jackson knew better. He'd always been a sucker for strong, self-willed women, and the fact he'd run into one who was struggling for control made it all the more interesting and, yes, amusing. His ex, Maggie, had control down to a science, which in retrospect was a joke because she'd left him for being too predictable.

A car passed, splashing rain water. It'd be predictable to brush Camille aside because of her unusual pastimes. Yes, it'd be predictable. He snapped his fingers. This time he'd show Maggie. Camille was attractive, with snappy, sporty hair that brought out the shape of her face. She had a slender body that looked like she was accustomed to exploring nature. Her style had an appeal, and he'd be a fool not to pursue her. Yes, a predictable fool.

Well, Maggie would see his unpredictability when she hunted him down to tell him whatever it was she'd called him about. Her rouge lips would form a slow cringe as realization of her mistake dawned. She'd panic and fight not to lose him. She would regret what she had lost. She would never guess he would forget her and go on with his career. She'd be withered when she found him hunting bears in Yellowstone and dating a very good-looking Camille. Now if only he could get Camille to go along with the plan for however long it took to get Maggie back.

———

Camille collapsed onto the living room couch when Jackson left. For some reason she couldn't stop rattling on and on about superstition. It wasn't healthy for her to keep focusing on it. She should stop. Why had she become so fixated on her fears lately? It being Halloween and her day having gone all wrong might be the reason.

Darlene walked into the room. "He's sure a nice guy. I can't believe he fixed our heater, made us a toasty hot fire, and now he's on his way to change our flat tire in the dark and rain."

"A full-fledged hero." Camille rubbed the kink in her neck.

"You've survived Halloween. Congratulations."

"Barely," Camille said.

"Let's see, you're forty-seven and you'll probably live to about eighty-five—"

"Eighty-five, heaven forbid—"

"So that means you have about thirty-eight more Halloweens and Friday the Thirteenths to go."

"I'm not talking about it."

And she didn't. Instead Camille retired to bed and slept soundly until she heard a banging in her head.

Boom. Boom. Boom. Over and over the tugging noise echoed. She groaned and plopped her pillow over her face. The pounding continued. Somewhere in the recesses of her mind, she computed that the noise wasn't a dream, but rather something outside. She sat up as the noise grew louder. She slipped off the bed, her feet gliding onto the chilled, wooden floor. Wrapping a robe around her, she guided her feet into pine needle–covered slippers. Silently she went down the stairs and flipped on the kitchen light. The sound stopped.

She poured herself a glass of milk and drank half the cup before the pounding resumed. Using the glowing lights from the appliances to make her way through the darkness, Camille rummaged through the few boxes that remained packed to find a miniature flashlight. She opened the door and walked outside. Almost immediately, her forehead smacked into something. "Ouch!" Rubbing her head, she twisted the base of the flashlight and pointed it at a ladder. Before she could think clearly, she heard someone singing, the banging drowning out the notes.

The noise came from the roof! To hear singing before breakfast was a sure sign of sorrow before nightfall. Plus, she'd walked under a ladder. Superstitious people would need to keep their fingers crossed until they saw a dog or three horses to undo the evil spell. *No, I don't believe it!* With her fingers defiantly uncrossed, she lifted her nightgown and bathrobe and climbed the ladder. Her flashlight darted around until it caught a dark form half a yard away. The light lingered on the vague object in the middle of the black soup. It had eyes. Brown.

"Get that thing out of my eyes," a voice boomed as an arm shot up over eyebrows for protection. "I can't see."

She lowered the light to focus on a long Roman nose. "Mind telling me what's going on up there?"

"I'm fixing your roof as we agreed. Remember? If I fix your tire, your roof, and get you heat, you agreed to take me to Yellowstone so I can shoot some bears. The tire's fixed, my truck's no longer around your tree, and your cabin's warm as promised. All that's left is to plug this hole."

"Couldn't it have waited until it's light?"

"Can't. I told you we have to leave early if I have any prayer of spotting a bear."

"How early?" She grabbed her robe tightly across her chest. She tried not to think how odd it was to be crouching on a leaky roof with a strange man.

"At three thirty. Sharp."

"What?" She wobbled from the sudden jerking movement and extended her arms to steady herself.

"Yep. That's cutting it close. And from what I know about you, things happen that gobble up time."

She turned and descended the ladder. Let him take her car. A simple answer. Never mind the fact that she needed to go to Yellowstone for research for her winter courses. Not to mention the history, the views, and the wildlife that beckoned. Then again, it would be nice to go there with someone who knew the area. She charged into the cabin, headed straight for the kitchen, and glanced at the microwave to check the time: 2:46 a.m. She needed to find out if Jackson was a safe person to travel with, and the Westguards were the only people she knew to ask. It was a bad time to call. They, of course, would be asleep, but Jackson insisted they leave at three thirty, and he'd be a stickler.

Whispering a prayer that the Westguards wouldn't be too upset, she dialed. A sleepy woman's voice floated over the phone line. "I'm sorry to wake you, Phyllis," Camille said, "but I really have an important question to ask."

"Whose cabin's on fire?"

"No one's."

"The Knowlands. Oh! Oh! Wake up, Bryson. The Knowlands' cabin is on fire. We gotta get there . . . I don't know, let me ask. How high are the flames?"

"There's no fire."

"What? I don't understand."

"This is Ms. Britain."

"The fire's quittin'?"

"No. Ms. Britain, the person who's staying in the Clarks' cabin."

"Oh, yes. The Skunk Lady."

What a label.

"How do you know the Knowlands' cabin is on fire? It's clear across the island from yours. You can't even see it from your place."

"No, I called to ask a question." Silence. Camille took a deep breath. "I need to know about Jackson Armstrong."

"You called at two in the morning to find out about Jackson?" The woman's voice reached a high pitch.

"You see, I'm supposed to leave with him for Yellowstone in an hour and my daughter's coming with me and I wanted—"

"You two are already dating? That's sweet. You make a lovely couple. He really needs to find a woman. I keep telling him, but he hasn't listened to me."

"It's not a date," Camille said, frustration seeping into her voice. "I want to know if Jackson's a safe guy. Do you know him very well?"

"Jackson? Our Jackson?" Phyllis laughed. "Heavens, yes. He'd never hurt a fly. Not even so much as raised a hand to his wife and, heaven knows, most men would've."

Like that would be okay, Camille thought.

"He might seem rough on the outside, but on the inside he's as tender as a new baby bird. Is that all, dear?"

"Yeah, thanks. Sorry for calling so early."

"You're very welcome. Call any time, but keep it after seven in the morning. And you two have fun on your date. There couldn't be a more romantic place than Yellowstone."

"It's not a date."

"Yes, yes, goodbye."

Camille frowned and hurried up the staircase. Darlene needed as much warning about leaving as possible. It was a struggle waking her daughter, but finally she managed. She rushed downstairs to prepare breakfast. She'd poured some checked-for-weevils-oats in boiling water when Darlene hopped downstairs with her hair combed and makeup on.

"I'm tired." Darlene sat at the table with a big yawn.

Camille set two bowls and spoons on the table. The banging picked up again.

"What's that noise?" Darlene asked. "I've been hearing it for hours."

"Jackson's fixing the roof."

"Cool. I'm going to invite him for breakfast." Darlene stood.

"I'm sure he's already eaten." Camille opened the refrigerator and pulled stuff out to make lunch. Maybe Jackson knew of a nice place they could have a picnic.

"I'll check."

Jackson accepted the invitation, and before Camille knew it, her daughter's nose was planted in a Yellowstone atlas. She flipped her hair over her shoulder and asked Jackson with a smile, "Are we really hunting bear?"

"Just to shoot pictures. We're not going to kill them."

"What kind are we looking for?"

"Black bears. They're the most common. I like going up to LeMar to search for them running between the trees."

"Is it scary? I mean . . . aren't you afraid of being attacked by one?"

Jackson flashed a large smile, apparently amused by Darlene's questioning or maybe her attention. He better not be a dirty old man. "There's a better chance of being struck by lightning," Jackson said. "Bear watching is perfectly safe."

"Oh, sure, sounds like it." Camille packed up the rest of the picnic lunch.

"Let's get going." He slapped his hands together and rubbed as if he was about to do something really exciting. "We're meeting a bear expert at five."

Darlene grabbed her purse off the table and threw on her jacket as she strode to the car. "Keys, Mom."

"Why?" Camille asked, not feeling in the mood for this game.

"I'm driving."

"Nope," Camille said.

"Why not?"

"'Cause I'm driving." Jackson approached them.

"I am," Camille said, "and that's final." She tried to slide between Jackson and Darlene by the staircase. They scooted together. "Excuse me," Camille said, "this is my car and I'm driving, thank you very much."

"But it's still dark. How about I drive so you two ladies can sleep?" Jackson asked.

She pushed herself past Jackson and her daughter and unlocked the door. "That's a mighty nice offer, but you're the one who didn't sleep." She slid into the driver's seat. Darlene shrugged and climbed in the back.

"Are you sure you don't want me to drive?" Jackson asked.

Camille started the car and shifted it into gear. Jackson grabbed his black bag off the ground as she inched forward. "Hey, wait a minute," he yelled. "I've got expensive camera gear here."

She waited until the front passenger door banged shut and then peeled out. She found she was crossing her fingers as she drove and forced herself to stop, noting that Jackson shot her hand a couple of odd glances before he wrinkled his nose. "I'm sorry, but it sure stinks in here."

It did smell like skunk, something she hoped to live down. She didn't say a thing. For some reason, having Jackson think of her as the stinky Skunk Lady bothered her. It shouldn't, of course, but to have anyone think of her as a person who smelled was humiliating.

She should rise above worrying about what others thought, and she would, too, she decided as she cracked the window to let the stink out. Wind rushed into the vehicle, creating a huge, obnoxious noise. She rolled the window back up. A truck passed them, and the headlights flashed inside the car, allowing Camille to see Jackson's face. His expression wasn't disgust, which she expected, but curiosity. Camille flushed deeply, wishing he hadn't looked at her like that. She felt as awkward as she had in her school days whenever a boy came near her. To her relief, Darlene changed the subject and kept the conversation bubbly, considering the time. "Where did you find a bear expert?" she asked Jackson.

"The Yellowstone Association can provide you with all sorts of neat stuff. You can even take classes. Some of them for college credit," Jackson said.

"Cool," Darlene said.

"Would you like to take that course?" Camille asked Darlene, trying not to act too hopeful.

"I don't know."

"There's plenty of things you can study for college credit around here," Jackson said. "My son takes all sorts of interesting classes."

"How old is your son?" Darlene questioned.

"Twenty-one."

"Does he look like you?"

"He's a mixture of his mom and me. Poor boy should've gotten all his mom's traits, then he'd be a looker."

"Oh, come on," Darlene said. "If he's anything like you, he's got to be hot."

Was she flirting? Camille cleared her throat. "Is there a store near this bear-watching place?" She darted a glance in the rearview mirror, hoping her daughter would see her look and realize telling a man who was old enough to be her father that he was "hot" was completely out of line.

"This is a national forest, not a drive-by-zoo," Jackson said.

Camille beamed red again. She was doing a great job making herself appear stupid in front of this cowboy. He must wonder how she ever got her doctorate degree. "What I meant was," she muttered, "how far will I have to drive to go to one of those tourist trap stores after I drop you off?"

"You won't be dropping me off. I thought you two would also like to watch the bears."

"Cool," Darlene said.

"But I need to put my course outline together," Camille said. "I have to find out if any of the stores around here sell obsidian." She stared out her windshield as if the solution to her problem would be solved by the trees whipping by. The headlights of the car danced yellow on the black road.

"What's obsidian?" Darlene asked.

"It's glass volcanic rock the Indians used to make tools from," Jackson said.

"How did you know that?" Camille glanced at him. He sat in the gray shadows of the car so she couldn't get a good read of his face.

"What? Do you think I don't know anything?"

Camille swallowed. "No."

"Then why the surprise?"

"I—I—I don't know. I guess you caught me off guard. I, ummm, thought that—" She had thought he wouldn't know anything. After all, he was a cowboy.

"Don't worry about it," Jackson said.

They drove in silence. The sun rose quickly, its golden rays erasing the velvety darkness on the mountains peak by peak. Camille snatched another glimpse of Jackson. The early morning sunlight highlighted him in his snug-fitting Levis and royal blue shirt, complementing the blond curls poking out of his cowboy hat. Large worn cowboy boots completed the ensemble. A man's man, Camille thought: tough, strong, and protective. A lot different from Adam, who was more of a thinker than a woodsman. It must be a very different experience to be married to someone like Jackson. Before she could think about that idea further, Darlene broke the silence by asking, "What color is obsidian?"

"Black," Camille answered.

"But there are some that are more unusual, tinted in red, brown, or green," Jackson said. "They're all over the stores. You shouldn't worry about finding them. It'll be no problem. On the way back, after I shoot my bear, we can stop."

"I bet they look cool," Darlene said.

They drove into another thick patch of pines. The slender, woody trees stood close together, forming prison-like bars on both sides of the road. Camille unbuttoned the top button on her flannel jacket, swallowing hard. "That's too nice of you," she said. "But we wouldn't want to put you out, so how about we drop you off at the bear place, and Darlene and I will dart over to Old Faithful? After we see the geyser spit and browse through the shops, we'll pick you up for lunch."

"But Mom, I want to see the bears," Darlene whined.

"That plan won't work," Jackson said.

"Why not?" Camille asked.

Jackson jumped into lecture mode. "First off, you don't drop people off and plan on picking them up later like it's a shopping mall. We're in a wilderness. And second, we're going north to LaMar to hunt bears. Old Faithful is south . . . What's the matter?" he asked her. "You city slickers scared of seeing bears?"

She refused to answer the jab, but to her dismay, Darlene continued the topic. "How scary is it?" She leaned up between Camille and Jackson.

"It's nothing. We won't even be getting close to them. You look in your binoculars or a spotting scope across a valley to another ledge."

"Doesn't sound so bad," Camille said.

"But how do you know the bears are going to stay on that side and not come over to the side we're on?" Darlene asked.

"You don't," Jackson answered. "The bears like to eat pine nuts and white bark off the trees. You can often find a few searching for food in the early morning . . ."

He talked on about bears, but Camille no longer listened. Darlene's question had spurred her into thought. How did a person know the bears, or potential danger of any kind, would stay over on the other side of the ravine? It was a question of safety. How did anyone truly know they were safe? Everyone wanted a guarantee. Camille knew she did when she had so trustingly given her heart to Adam. She had assumed that the instructions, "Handle with care," would be a given. Adam was supposed to have seen her heart's worth and not take it lightly. Maybe he had a glimpse of the gift at the beginning, but as time wore on, he grew complacent and thoughtless, and perhaps thought the danger wasn't real. This idea startled Camille. Could Adam have been hurt and scarred from their breakup too? Did the danger only attack her heart or had Adam's heart been hurt?

Darlene's voice broke into her thoughts. "What causes bear

attacks?" Camille refocused on their conversation, curious for the answer.

"Different reasons," Jackson said. "The most common is they're scared. The best way not to threaten them is to go limp and curl up in a ball to protect your soft spots. Make slow movements. Talk, using a calm, unrushed voice."

So bears attack because they're scared, Camille thought. Destruction most often came out of fear. That idea worked as a concept, but did it work for her situation? Could Adam have been scared with her heart and not known what to do with it? Could she have been scared too? Did they not learn how to protect their love in case of an attack? She was now protecting herself, coming out here, staying away from him and the pain. She had taken enough risks lately, surviving her metaphorical bear attack, and now would consider herself foolish if she took another unneeded chance.

"I bet another reason bears attack is to protect their young," Darlene added. Her daughter sounded excited about this stuff. Jackson had mentioned his son took college courses around here. Maybe—just maybe—she could get her daughter into one of those classes.

"You've got a smart one here," Jackson said.

Maybe he wasn't so bad. Camille waited for him to gaze out the window before giving him another look. What was the appeal? He wasn't a drop-dead gorgeous kind of guy, but he wasn't ugly. Definitely all man. Hardy and rough—and something stirred in her when he was around.

"They become more aggressive," Jackson was saying. He sure seemed knowledgeable about this area. That could become an asset in helping outline her course. She shook her head. No.

"What's the superstition behind bears?" he asked.

Was he making fun of her? "What makes you think there is one?"

"There has to be. Out with it."

Camille flinched, again wishing she didn't have this overwhelming compulsion to always answer people's questions. She'd have to overcome that hang-up, but for now, she gave in, too tired to stand up to him. "The English thought bears only bred once every seven years and when they did, there was trouble. It was a sign of bad luck to the other animals that were breeding. People would know when a bear had a cub because a baby cow would suddenly die or a cat litter would be found dead. There's also a legend about a soldier who tried to kill a bear while guarding the Tower of London and the bayonet went right through the bear with no harm done to the animal, but the man fell down in a fit and died."

"Are there any good superstitions?" Darlene asked, yawning.

"One. If a child rode on the back of a bear, it'd keep him from whooping cough, or if he caught it, he'd be cured."

"We need to ride on the back of a bear," Jackson said, "although bears normally breed every two to three years."

"I never said I believed the superstition. I just said the English people used to believe it." Up ahead, a large vehicle was parked off in the distance. The closer she came, the more it appeared to be a truck. Her headlights shone on the truck, and she could see there was something in the back. She eased her foot off the gas.

"A dog!" Darlene yelled. "Stop. Someone's left that poor dog outside to starve."

"I'm sure someone's sleeping in the truck," Camille said.

"Stop," Jackson said.

"What? You too?" Camille asked.

"It looks like my son's truck."

Before the car came to a complete stop, both Jackson and Darlene bolted from the car.

She was traveling with two lunatics.

CHAPTER SIX

Camille's hand lingered on the keys before she turned off the ignition. The black sky lightened as faint golden rays migrated upwards. This time of day was the best hour for a child to be born. It meant the babe would have a better chance of reaching old age; the later in the day, the shorter the life. Darlene had come at high noon, Camille remembered, grabbing her purse. Peering through the dark mist and clenching her hands, she approached the truck. Two shadows leaned toward the driver's side in a huddle—Jackson and Darlene. She picked up her pace, shoes clicking along the paved road. "What's going on?"

Jackson gestured toward the passenger inside the car. "This is my boy, Austin. Austin, this is Ms. Britain and her daughter Darlene. They're living in the Clarks' cabin."

Camille nodded a hello as Jackson added, "I thought you were coming next week." The boy looked up with big brown eyes so much like his father's. "I decided to surprise ya and come earlier. Cool, huh?"

"The truth?" Jackson asked.

Austin smiled until his dimples indented. "A camping trip. It would've been awesome. We were going to hike the Fountain Point

Pot Natural Trail in Geyser Country to see the mud pots and the waterfalls, but those wimps bagged out because of the rain."

"I'm surprised you didn't go anyway," Jackson muttered. Then, as though giving it thought, he asked, "You didn't, did you?"

"What's wrong if he did?" Darlene asked.

"Ah, little honey—" Jackson said.

Darlene frowned. "I'm not little, and I'm not your honey."

Jackson didn't let this bother him but continued with what he was going to say. "Every year Search and Rescue has to look for lost hikers. A couple of years ago some teens fell into a geyser. The girl died, and the boys suffered third degree burns. It's not something you mess with. The number one rule of survival is never go alone and always inform people where you'll be, right son?"

"Um, yeah. Whatever."

Jackson's eyes bore into his son like mini lie detectors. After getting a reading on Austin, he said, "You went by yourself. How many times do I have to tell you?" He kept his voice even, as if the lecture was routine, something he engaged in more out of habit than with feeling.

Camille could identify. She experienced similar episodes with Darlene on a regular basis. It made her wonder why she and Jackson wasted their breath. Their children would do whatever stupid thing they wanted, no matter what their parents said.

"Dad, I don't need lectures," Austin said.

"You do if you keep making the same dumb mistakes."

Austin ran his hand through his brown hair. "Chill. It was only one night, and I didn't go very far. I didn't even stay for more than a couple of hours 'cause your warning kept going through my head driving me crazy. So there. I hiked out, started driving home, got tired, and pulled over to the side of the road for sleep. Happy?"

"Yes," Jackson said.

Camille was satisfied too. Kids actually did hear lectures—well, at least sometimes. She looked over at her daughter, who pretended not to pay attention to the scene as she petted a taffy-colored, long-haired dog in the bed of the truck. "What's his name?" Darlene asked.

"Rusty." Austin grabbed the dog's thick jaw. The golden retriever lavished his face with his tongue.

"Um, Austin, we're on our way to Lamar to shoot bears for my magazine job. Like to come?" Jackson asked.

"Sure. Already had my run-in with bears, but I'm brave enough to do it again."

"Yeah, right," Darlene said.

"I am."

"What about Rusty?" Camille asked. "There's not enough room."

"My mom's afraid of dogs," Darlene blurted. "No, more like petrified."

Jackson cocked an eyebrow in a questioning manner.

"I never liked animals." Camille flushed, wishing she didn't feel compelled to answer the nonverbal questions people asked too.

"Ah, Rusty wouldn't hurt a skunk." Jackson laughed at his own joke, which Camille didn't find at all amusing. After composing himself, he said, "I have an idea. Why don't Darlene and Austin take Rusty back to my cabin, put him in the garage, and catch up with us for lunch in Cody? It was founded by Buffalo Bill. That should be enough history for your liking." Jackson winked at Camille.

"Dad, he'll freeze in the garage."

"Why don't you let him in the house?" Darlene asked.

"My dad is allergic to him," Austin said. "I mean, he can stand him for a bit, but not when the hair and stuff gets all over the house."

"He could ride with Austin in the truck and follow us," Camille said.

"Great," Jackson said. "Darlene, you ride with Austin. If he gets tired, you can take over."

"I'll take over now." Darlene extended her hand for the keys.

"Not on your life," Austin said.

"Don't tell me you're one of those sexist-type guys who believes in being in complete control? You know, the kind that'll freak out if they can't operate a remote?"

Austin puffed out his chest in fake pride. "No one drives my truck but me. Girl or boy."

Camille leaned over to get a better look at this "hot" vehicle. A big jacked-up four-by-four, high enough to require two steps to climb in. A large roll bar with huge fog lights. Great. Definitely a wild type. She eyed the teenager. His light brown hair was feathered on top, with a short trim by his ears. His brown eyes glimmered—sensual like his father's—his nose small and delicate. He must've inherited that from his mom. Overall, nice looking. A kid Darlene might fall for.

Jackson slapped his hands together. "Stop the lollygagging and let's go. I need to shoot me a bear."

The group dispersed. Camille and Jackson walked back to her car together.

"Keys?" He extended his hand. "I like control." He dashed her a smile.

It felt like a cold glass of water on parched lips to have someone willingly admit a weakness. Besides, she was sick of driving. Her hand released the keys to the huge, extended palm. That was when she noticed that one of his fingers still wore a gold band.

———

The keys clinked as they fell into his father's hands. *Odd that Dad had to ask Camille if he could drive,* Austin thought. His mother would have handed him the keys when she first saw him. And there was something more he didn't like about Camille—and Darlene too, for that matter. Neither one of them wore much makeup or looked done up. Darlene did have long shiny hair, but her bossy attitude covered up the merits of her hair.

"Don't slam my door," he mumbled to Darlene, but his eyes fixed on the car ahead of him, where Camille climbed in to sit next to his dad.

"I wouldn't dream of it," Darlene said.

Austin knew she swam in sarcasm, but it would be best if he didn't respond, so he simply revved the engine before tailgating his father. With his headlights on, there was no way his father would forget that he was driving right behind him, even for a brief second. He refused to let his father forget about his family. "Is your mom married?" he asked.

"My parents got divorced about six months ago," Darlene said. "How long have your parents been divorced?"

He flinched. He hated the idea of that word directed at his family. Their divorce had gone through, but that didn't mean it was permanent. He hated the idea of their family being broken—and especially the idea of his mother being single. His buddies had joked with him about how stupid his dad was to let anyone as hot as his mom go. Austin had already been in more than one fight from other comments his friends had made about his mom. They shouldn't look at his mother that way. If he had his wish, he'd deck anyone who did. "Technicality," he grumbled.

"So how long has it been?"

"A few weeks, maybe. But my dad has made it absolutely clear he plans to win my mom back. We talk about it all the time." Austin released some of the pressure he was applying to the gas pedal. His father had already braked twice.

Darlene twisted a strand of hair. "Do you think he'll be successful?"

"Yeah. My dad never gives up. I know he loves her more than anything. That's the point."

Brown meadows with distant rolling mountains spread out before them, along the paved road they drove on. When his mother came here to find his dad, as she promised she would, his parents couldn't help but rekindle their romance in such a setting. Darlene sounded skeptical because her parents' marriage had failed. Her mom wasn't meant to be with her father, but his parents were meant to be together. They complimented each other perfectly. When his dad was still living in Denver and he came out for visitations, it became apparent to Austin how much they fit together. He never mentioned it, but his father would take him to the same spaghetti factory as his mom took him to the night before. Both parents would comment that it was the best restaurant around, and then they would each order the same dish. They would go to the same music concerts, not knowing the other person was there. But Austin knew.

––––––

The gray sky surrounded their car as they drove toward the West Yellowstone entrance gate. Traveling through the early morning took Camille back to a family trip she'd taken with Adam and the kids. They'd driven to Lake Powell in the middle of the night, wanting to spend as much time as possible camping, hiking, and water-skiing. She had envisioned long, fun-filled, sunny days and dreamed about how they would maneuver the boat through the ruffling waves, laughing as the breeze raced across them.

Hours would be spent encouraging and teaching their children how to put pressure on the back foot of the ski so they'd pop out of the water. Then they'd hike through the red cliffs and stop at a shaded grove for a picnic. Best of all, in the evenings, maybe she and Adam would leave the children at camp and take a private ride through the water. They'd find a remote spot, she'd relax into his arms, and they'd rediscover their love for each other. It had been a long time since they had given their relationship that kind of nurturing.

Unfortunately, the reality had been much different. The first day consisted mostly of sharp orders to fix up the camp, and then Adam left with the kids for a short ride as she prepared dinner. After she cleaned up from their evening meal, she found him in an exhausted heap, snoring. The second day went no better. There was always work for her to do, and he was always off with the kids, hiking and boating. When all the meals and cleanup had been done, he said, "I'm taking Richard fishing. We'll be home later."

"But I thought . . ." Camille had let her protest trail off.

By the next to last day, she had reached her breaking point. He had a map and water jug in hand when she stopped him. "We need to talk," she demanded. "Now." She would take no excuse; the nonsense had gone on long enough.

"What?" he said, tapping his map against his knee.

The tapping sounded in her brain over and over. Tap, tap, tap, hurry, hurry, hurry.

"Sometimes I get the feeling I don't exist," she said. She waited for him to say, "Don't be silly. You're my life." Then he'd squeeze her tight and she'd believe him.

Instead he said, "I've just taken a whole week off from work. A week I couldn't afford—and you're complaining? Cam, I give up. You're impossible to please." He packed up their stuff in a controlled, rapid motion, then drove them home. They'd screeched to a halt in front of their average, brown brick house before the sun had set on the day, never to go on a family vacation or any trip together again. Sometime around then, he must've fallen out of love with her.

"Whach'ya thinking over there?" Jackson's voice broke into her wounded feelings.

"Nothing."

"Tell me."

The silence was thick between them. A square block of pain a hand's width above her stomach knotted, throbbed, and twisted. All the hurt, rejection, and humiliation had been shoved into that tight box. She needed to feel it, share it, expose the hurt for healing. But the risk might be too great.

"I'm just remembering." She choked on the word that was coated with unwanted emotion.

"From the tone of your voice, they aren't good memories." He was inviting her to share, and it seemed that he cautiously, gently, oozed with kindness. A passing vehicle's headlights shone in the car, illuminating Jackson's face as he watched her. Camille saw the concern.

Then she remembered.

The gold band.

He was married.

That settled it. She really didn't want to bare her soul to a man who had told her he had an ex-wife and yet clearly had some attachment to her. And yet . . . "I thought you were divorced." Camille pointed at the gold band.

His cheeks reddened. "I—I . . . oh." His hand patted the steering wheel. "She left me." It was his turn to have his voice crack and fill with emotion. "I guess I was thinking that maybe . . ." His throat muscles flinched. Crimson covered his face.

"I'm sorry," Camille said.

They drove on in silence. Camille watched the clock numbers change on the dashboard. Finally, she said, "I've been thinking about what went wrong in my marriage. It started out so well and ended so poorly." Tears came, as she knew they would. "I feel like such a failure."

"Did he tell you why he left?" he asked before hurriedly adding, "I apologize. I shouldn't have asked that. It was wrong for me to assume he was the one that left. Oh, I mean, I shouldn't have asked. I mean, ah—"

"It's okay. I've needed to talk about it, and it might as well be to a stranger." She leaned her head against the headrest, thinking it odd that out of everyone who had offered to listen to her, she had chosen him, this stranger, this cowboy.

For another long moment they were silent. Then he spoke. "Uh, you were going to tell me about his reasons for leaving," he prompted.

"I don't think I want to tell you that."

"I'll give you my ex-wife's reason after you tell me."

"Promise?"

"Promise."

"Adam—that's my ex—said we were two strangers living together, going through the motions, and that we didn't even know each other."

"Was he right?"

"At first I felt he'd blindsided me in the back of the head with a big two-by-four, but now—I don't know. We definitely drifted apart. How were we supposed to be this close couple who knew each other inside and out, when he was always off trading stocks?"

"I can't help but think my marriage would've been saved if I wasn't home as much as I was," Jackson said. "She got to know me too well, and then she thought I was—" It was his turn to trail off into painful memories.

"Was what?"

"Predictable." His voice cracked.

"Predictable?" She laughed. "You're anything but that. I mean, heaven sakes, I woke up with hammering on my roof at two in the morning and now we're chasing bears. You're quite the adventurer."

Jackson's smile flowed right into her heart and lasted until they made their way to the entrance of Yellowstone. The line to get in was nonexistent. She sat up taller in her seat as the admittance clerk handed them a free map and pamphlets. "I can't believe I'm finally here."

He smiled. "Is this a big dream?"

"You could say that," she answered. She buried her hand in her purse, fumbling through her pencils, pens, and tissues until she found a flashlight. The day had lightened up, but it still wasn't bright enough to see the printed word. Twisting the end piece of the flashlight, she lit the pamphlet and thumbed through the pages. "Where are we going?"

"Lamar Valley."

She unfolded the map, flipping the light over it. "We came in the west gate, right?"

"Lamar is up north and east."

Her flashlight scanned the red lines on the map. After going over it carefully three different times, she asked, "Where?"

"I thought you'd never ask. Lamar's right—" He leaned over to point.

She snatched the paper away. "I'll do it myself," she said, not liking his condescending tone. She continued to look over the sites as Jackson chuckled. Eventually she did manage to find Lamar. "Here it is. Not very big, is it?"

"It doesn't have to be a big tourist site for bears." He flipped on a country radio station, the volume low. "Actually, Fishing Bridge used to be a major tourist area. The park's closing it down. They built it before biologists realized they'd built on a major bear spot."

"You'd think they would have figured that out before they started building," Camille said.

"A government agency is a government agency."

She chuckled. "Isn't that the truth."

"Don't you mean ain't?" He'd referred to yesterday. A day she never wanted to remember. "Did I offend you?" he asked. "Maybe I should exercise some mince in my language."

"Mince?"

"Yes, mince. It means to use restraint with words to the bound of decorum," he said, laughing.

"I deserved that. I was a fool yesterday. You must think I'm the worst oaf you've ever met."

"Oaf? That's an interesting word choice."

"I know it's dated, but it's the best description I can come up with."

"You shouldn't feel that way. We all have bad days."

"Mine happen to arrive every Halloween and Friday the Thirteenth."

"Superstition doesn't explain that."

She stared at him, and he turned his gaze to her. His brown eyes reflected something she couldn't quite pinpoint. Anger? Irritation? Hurt? She was unsure and felt tremendous relief when he looked away. "What makes you so sure?" she asked.

"My mom was a fanatic about that stuff."

"Like how?"

He didn't answer her for a long time, and when he did, his voice had grown sharp and terse. "I don't want to talk about it." That statement chilled the conversation. Jackson must have noticed her discomfort because he said, "Sorry. Just more bad memories."

"That's fine." She tapped the map. "Anyway, I was wondering what some interesting sites are to watch for."

"We don't have time to stop."

"Okay, then, can you tell me what I'm missing?"

"Sure. The biggest thing would probably be Mammoth Hot Springs. They have incredible travertine terraces that make you feel like you've died and gone to heaven."

"That pretty, huh?"

"Yeah, and the fact that all the mountains are white. It's really something when clouds come and settle on them. The old name for Mammoth was White Mountains."

"Why'd they change it?"

"I don't know."

"I bet there were lots of mammoths around this area," Camille said. "Can you imagine hunting one of those huge beasts? Indians must've had nerves of stone. I could never have done it."

"You're underestimating yourself. You could do it if it meant feeding your family."

Mountains loomed around them protectively, and she felt an increase in her pulse from his compliment. In an effort to gain control over the nerves pounding inside her head, she crossed her legs. The map slid. She grabbed at it. "What else am I missing?"

"Nothing."

With her flashlight, she followed the thin, dark-red line on the map that represented the road they were traveling. "Ah, Sheepeaters' Cliff. That must be quite a view. Do they think that's where the Sheepeaters stayed?"

"I don't know anything about it. I only know I haven't felt this alive in years." He guided the car onto the shoulder of the road.

"Are we already there?" Camille asked with a high pitch.

He glanced into her hazel eyes and smiled. His eyes went to her hair, and she wondered if it looked funny or something. "Nope."

"Then what we are doing?" She pulled her cardigan tighter around her.

"Come on." He climbed out of the car.

"What's going on? Is something wrong?" Austin asked, coming from the truck behind them to Camille's side of the car. His father opened the back door of the car.

"It's beyond me," Camille said. "You'll have to ask your father. He's acting mysterious."

"Not that mysterious. Will all of you walk to the pine tree that's being swallowed up by the fir?"

"I'd rather be shot over there." Darlene pointed to a tree about four feet in front of the Britain's car.

"If I have to die," Austin said, "kill me in front of my truck."

"Isn't that obsessive?" Darlene asked. "Wanting to die with your vehicle by your side?"

"Not by my side, behind me," Austin said.

Jackson set up the camera equipment, smiling as Camille watched.

The group gathered close, Camille standing in the middle with Darlene on one side and Austin on the other where Jackson would join him. He pressed the timer and rushed to stand behind Austin, squeezing his head in between Camille and his son. Camille was looking at him when the flash snapped, and she saw him wink at the camera. "Thank you, guys. Now back to the bears."

After getting back into the car, Camille asked, "What was that little excursion?"

"I want to remember the trip."

"You could've done it when we got to the site."

"That's predictable."

She laughed. "You're anything but that."

Jackson looked pleased. He looked at Camille again and smiled, sending a flush of heat through her body. Maybe she'd also want to have a picture to remember this day.

———

When he'd collected his camera material, Jackson flipped on his cell phone so he could check if Maggie had called again. With everything happening so fast, he hadn't had time to call her back. That was only half true. He could've made some excuse and given her a quick call, but he wasn't sure if he was up for that yet. What would he say to her? He carried his camera equipment into the trunk as he dialed his voice messages, but his cell phone was still searching for a signal. He'd have to try again later. Maggie wouldn't like it if he didn't respond soon.

He paused before slamming shut the trunk, seeing Camille standing by the passenger door. She looked exquisite. It would be nice to have just a picture of her alone. She didn't see him as predictable. She wasn't at all like Maggie, and he was enjoying being with her more than he would admit.

He took the shot and winked at her as she blinked in surprise. "I couldn't resist," he said.

She flushed, looking even prettier. *This,* Jackson thought, *is working up to be a pretty good day.*

———

Darlene climbed into the car and slammed the door. "Your dad's a real creep."

Austin shot her an irritated glance. He was in no mood for this. "Why do you say that?"

"Don't tell me you don't know, Mr. He's-Going-To-Get-Back-Together-With-My-Mom!" She flicked the vanilla-scented Christmas tree hanging from the rearview mirror.

"He is."

"If he loves your mother and plans to marry her again, then he has some nerve carrying on with *my* mom!"

"Sorry, Ms. Moral Police, but your mom shouldn't be batting her eyes at him. For heaven's sakes, she's old enough to be a mom." Austin stopped the Christmas air freshener from swinging.

"She is a mom."

"Proves my point."

"You have no point. It was your dad who put his arm around her for the picture. And what was all that at the car about not being able to resist taking her picture?"

"I bet she cast a womanly spell on him." He revved up the engine again.

"Womanly spell?"

"You know what I'm talking about. That spell you girls use as a secret weapon against us poor, innocent men."

"Well, Mister-Know-It-All, how does it work?"

"I don't know. I told you it was a secret. All the women in the world have banded together and promised not to tell any male the source of its power."

Darlene rolled her eyes. "Would you get real? It's your dad causing the trouble."

"What's he done?"

"Like you don't know. He's leading my mom on, telling her he's free when he's not. If he's planning to get back with your mom, he has no business taking pictures of my mom and staring at her like a lovesick cow. Hardly innocent behavior if you ask me."

Austin pressed his foot on the gas and tore down the road.

"What are you doing?" Darlene grasped the dashboard.

"Having a little fun."

"Come on, slow down."

"Are you chicken?" He swerved in front of his dad's car.

"Not in the slightest." She squared her shoulders. "I can handle anything you dish out."

"Are you sure?"

"Positive."

He pressed on the gas as the truck shifted gears. The speedometer inched up higher as the truck shook. Loud, long honking blared from Camille's car. Austin looked through the back window and saw their parents signaling them to stop.

"You better let them in front," Darlene said.

"Calling it quits?" he asked, taking his foot off the gas petal.

"Heck no. I have nerves of steel. I'll challenge you to a new competition."

"Like what?" Austin asked.

"Don't know."

He grinned. "I'll find something. But until then, why don't we call a truce and stop fighting about our parents?"

"Why?"

"'Cause we both want the same thing. We could work together."

"What is it we both want?"

"For our parents not to get together." Austin looked at Darlene. She was so hot when she was happy, and when she was angry, with her long hair bouncing, she was completely irresistible. His girlfriend back home wouldn't like him going to Yellowstone with someone this attractive.

"Deal. What do you have in mind?"

"I'm not sure yet, but we'll come up with something."

———

"We're here."

Jackson's voice held an anxious excitement, but the words had a different effect on Camille. Panic seemed to swell and bubble inside her. What if they got too close to the bears? What if the bears sensed her fear and it drew them to her like moths to a porch light?

"Their feeding ground is across the gully," he said. Soothing reassurance seemed to radiate from him.

This startled Camille. His words and looks peered into her soul as though he could read her mind. No, that wasn't exactly right. He had the ability to connect with her soul, knowing her inner vulnerabilities, and he studied her weakness like a doctor examining symptoms, compiling a prescription for her, as well as treating her with his gaze. He gave her a blend of compassion and harmony.

The combination immediately seeped into her being and relieved her ache, vanquishing her fear and replacing it with subtle calmness. This experience surprised Camille. How could this man see inside her with such understanding? Did he have a magical ability to see more than the trappings of her physical body? He seemed to break right through all her barriers, making his way around her hurts, flaws, and weaknesses to find her core, her goodness. Respect and honor flowed from him as if he'd found a glorious light, a glorious being, buried inside her. Baffled, Camille stood frozen, struck as a jet of energy hit her. She didn't reject it as would be her normal impulse. Instead, she accepted the honor and respect he gave her, unashamed.

"Wow!" She thought she heard him whisper. Heat exploded through her, but she was lost and didn't know how to respond. She ended up not doing anything because at that moment Darlene flopped her arm around her, tugging her forward, straight through a clump of sage.

"Excuse us," her daughter said to Jackson, "we need to go hunting for the little girl's room."

Before Camille could get a word out, they staggered far enough away from Jackson that unless Camille yelled, he wouldn't hear anything she said. Had she imagined the understanding and compassion she felt from him? Never before had she experienced anything like that. Why had she experienced such a connection with him, of all people?

She wrapped her hand around her daughter's slender frame, abruptly remembering her earlier concern. "Mind telling me what you were thinking when you told a man who's old enough to be your father that he's 'hot?'"

"What?" Darlene asked, using a sarcastic trill. "You can't tell me you haven't noticed, Ms. Blush."

This jab caught Camille up short. Her daughter was baiting, trying to redirect her attention. Time to shuffle a sidestep. "Why was Austin driving like a madman? Was he trying to get you killed?"

"Gee, Mom, relax. You're always overacting. He was just showing off what his truck could do."

They talked on about young adults and their impulses until they returned to where Austin and Jackson waited for them. A ranger was pointing at a group of trees. "Just saw some grizzlies feeding down in that terrain yesterday. I'm sure they're still around."

Camille stepped up to Jackson, watching his reaction. He seemed genuinely pleased to see her. He gave her a sideways glance. Suddenly she was bumped and had to take a step back to maintain her balance. It was Darlene, who had squeezed between her and Jackson. Why would she do that? Normally, she'd be excited to play matchmaker.

"Dad," Austin said. He squatted several yards away near a clump of pine trees, fiddling with the camera equipment. "I need your help."

Darlene tugged Camille's arm. "Mom, why don't we ditch these two? They have a car. They don't need us."

"I thought you wanted to see a bear."

"I do. I mean for us to leave after we see one."

"What's the problem? Did something bad happen between you and Austin? Did he—?"

"Calm down. Nothing bad happened. Austin's nice enough, but I think we'd have more fun together—just you and me."

Something wasn't right. "But I thought you'd enjoy having someone around your age. Not to mention good looking."

"He's not that cute."

"Oh, come on. You were telling me how gorgeous his father was, and Austin looks just like him—only a younger, improved version."

Darlene struggled to hide any reaction but failed miserably.

"I can tell you agree," Camille said. "I'd have better luck on my research if we travel with someone who knows about the place. Let's stick around for a while."

Jackson signaled to her. She joined him, and Darlene trudged behind her. When she reached the men, Jackson handed her a pair of binoculars and gave another set to her daughter.

"We'll be safe, I promise," Jackson whispered close to Camille's ear. A shiver spread through her from the faint, warm touch of his breath.

"Hey, Dad," Austin said, sliding between the two of them.

"What?"

"What kind of film do you want me to put in? The two hundred or four?"

"Two. You know that."

"Time for bear watching," the ranger said. "Keep your eyes on the trees."

"How do you know what to look for?" Camille asked.

"Black spots. They'll be hunting for pine nuts. A crucial food source this time of year."

"Why?" Darlene asked.

"It gives them fat for hibernation," Austin answered.

Camille glanced at Austin, thinking that it wouldn't hurt to be nice. "You know about bears, too?"

"I'm taking classes from the Yellowstone Institute."

"That's right, your father told us," Camille said. "What kind of classes can you take?"

"All types. Canoeing, mammal tracking, photography, bird calls, the Nez Perce, wolves, history of the park, ecosystem, and, of course, bear watching."

Camille observed Darlene to see if there was any sign of interest.

Her daughter's face held a blank stare. "Interesting subjects. Do you like them?" Camille asked Austin.

"They're cool. The best thing about them is I get to learn the things I want and receive college credit."

"What's your major?"

"Not sure yet. I'm thinking about business or law."

"Wow. That's a long way from those courses," Camille said.

"I know, but a scientist or ranger doesn't really rake in the bucks. There's a cabin at Bill's Island that I'm going to buy someday. It's huge. Have you seen it?"

"I don't know," Camille answered.

"You'd know it if you saw it. It's on the waterfront and has blue stones and a huge royal blue roof. It also has deck after deck after deck. The decks curl around like a snake down to the beachfront. I'm telling you, I'm going to own it. They have a big barbecue pit, tetherball, volleyball, and a huge swing set area. I'm going to live there and go waterskiing in the early morning, wolf- and buffalo-watching in the late morning, motorcycling the rest of the day, and snow skiing and snowmobiling in the winter."

"Sounds like the life," Darlene said.

His chest expanded. "I'll have it, too."

"Yeah, right." Darlene said.

Jackson eyed Camille. "Have you seen the cabin he's talking about?"

"Nope."

"It's a couple of cabins down from yours. You should go on a walk just to see it. It's a masterpiece. Looks like it could be a hotel. A very nice one."

"Then I'll go see it," Camille said, smiling at Jackson. She found herself wanting to ask him if he'd walk there with her, but Darlene's frown made her change her mind.

The group spent the next half hour in silence as they searched for bears, but apparently bad luck still plagued Camille, and in turn the whole group. None of them saw even a hint of a bear. The ranger gave up with a shrug. "They must've moved on. They like Hayden Valley. Maybe you should try there."

"We'll do that," Jackson said.

"Hayden Valley," Camille said. "Is that by chance named after Dr. Ferdinand V. Hayden who led an expedition there with Thomas Moran and William Henry Jackson?"

"Right on," the ranger answered.

"I love Moran's paintings. They're breathtaking. No wonder they stirred the hearts of lawmakers into protecting this park."

The ranger smiled. "I loved them too. The way he utilized the light in his landscapes is incredible. His use of colors ranged from those so light they barely exist to the very bright I'm-here-notice-me colors."

Camille laughed. "He was good." She hooked her arm around Jackson's and said, "Come on, what are we waiting for? Let's go to Hayden Valley."

"Mom, can I ride with you?" Darlene asked.

"Shhh, Darlene," Camille whispered. "Don't be rude."

"That's okay." Austin smiled. "I'd like to spend time with my dad. It's been a long while since we've seen each other."

Camille released her hold on Jackson's arm. Why had she grabbed him? It had seemed so natural.

Jackson patted her shoulder. "'Til Hayden then." She nodded and returned to her car but stopped before opening the door and ran back to Jackson.

"What? Can't stand to be away from me?" he asked with a wink.

"You have my keys."

"Oh." He dug in his pocket.

He was so tall, with such broad shoulders. It felt comfortable to be near him. Why comfortable? She'd never felt that with Adam. She'd experienced electricity, frustration, and excitement, but never comfort.

"Here you go." He handed her the keys. Their hands briefly touched. Warmth rushed through her as if she'd wrapped herself in a homemade quilt. Where were the nervous butterflies that so often made her nauseated?

"Let me drive, Mom." Darlene stood in front of the driver's side of the car with her hand extended. Camille handed the keys over like a robot.

Once they pulled onto the road to Hayden, Camille opened her map and studied it. "Remind me that I want to see Tower Falls on the way home."

"What is it?" Darlene asked.

"A huge volcanic mountain with two water falls spilling off it. I read in one of the early explorer's journals about their amazement over how loud the pumping water was. It was so noisy they couldn't hear each other shouting."

"Umm," Darlene said.

"Thomas Moran died with an unfinished painting of the Tower Falls on his easel. He loved both it and place called Inspiration Point. I wonder where it's located?" Camille returned her attention to the map.

"Mom, I think you're getting too friendly with that Jackson guy."

Camille continued devouring the map, searching for Inspiration Point. "Don't worry. Yesterday you encouraged me to get to know him better, and now you're changing your mind. It's okay. I understand. It's hard for kids, even grown-up kids, to see their parents have a life outside of taking care of them. It'll take some getting used to."

"Mom, it's not that."

"Then what is it?"

"Well . . ."

"What?"

"I don't like him. He doesn't seem trustworthy."

"I appreciate your concern, but it's not like I'm going to marry the guy. We're just going to spend a day in the park. Then we'll return to our separate cabins. That's it."

"But Mom—"

"I have to tell you, though, I find it refreshing to talk to a man other than your father. I've been so angry with men that it's been really hard to open up and talk to anyone. Jackson understands, since he's going through something similar. But as a love interest?" Her speech faded away.

"What, Mom?"

"He's not for me."

"Why?"

"I don't want to sound snobby, but . . ." She stopped, her thoughts trailing to the feeling she'd had with Jackson. Had it been all in her imagination?

"But you're going to sound snobby. So out with it."

"Well, Jackson's a friendly guy and all, but he's too hick for me."

"What do you mean, hick?"

"Cowboy."

"Are you too stuffy to be involved with a cowboy?"

"It's not that." Camille stared out the window into the golden cast that the sun shone on the native grasses.

"What is it?"

Camille rubbed her fingers as she thought. "If I ever get involved again, it's going to be with the perfect man. It caused too much pain and sorrow to be mixed up with the wrong type."

"What's your type?"

"Smart. Very, very smart. A thinker. Someone who reflects, who's into philosophy, theater, and history. Someone who could get lost in a museum and spend hours reflecting on the past."

"That sounds like you," Darlene said.

"Exactly. I want a perfect match."

"Boooorrrring!" Her daughter yawned long and exaggerated while tapping her hand over her open mouth.

"Okay, little Miss Know-It-All, what's your perfect guy?"

"Cute—definitely has to have the looks. Muscular, smart, rich, fun."

"Get more specific."

"Fine. He has to know what he wants and have the guts to get it, letting no one stand in his way. He must love life and not be one of those drones who complains about everything. And he has to be unpredictable. I want surprises at every turn."

"Sounds scary."

"Well, yours is definitely boring."

"Not boring," Camille said. "Comfortable. Nice. I'm too old to long for adventure. I just want someone to sit with me, reflecting on life, while sipping tea in front of the setting sun."

"That definitely wouldn't fit Jackson."

"My point exactly."

CHAPTER SEVEN

As they drove in the car, Camille had become immersed in the sedges waving in the breeze and in a few large gray stones dotting the land when she noticed Austin's truck pulled over onto the side of the road. Austin's face peered through his back window, pointing to a herd of grazing elk.

"Look at them," Camille said as Darlene weaved the car onto the gravel that lined the road. The huge animals stretched across the meadow, nibbling on the grasses. Their dark heads, necks, and legs stood out as their creamy rumps blended into the surroundings. Antlers lurched out in massive grandeur, daring anyone to mess with them or their chosen gal.

"There's sure a lot of them."

"They travel in herds for protection. Before the Europeans arrived, the naturalists estimated there were ten million elk in North America. Now the scientists think there's only a million," Camille said.

"Whew! That's terrible. I can't believe what we've done—"

Camille interrupted before Darlene could lament any more about animal injustices. "There was a wildlife site on the Internet that said twenty-five percent of the elk are right here in Yellowstone. So we evil humans have done some good in protecting the wildlife."

"Glad to hear it," Darlene said, rolling her eyes. "But it's not enough."

Camille brushed a long strand of Darlene's hair off her face. "Didn't mean to steal your thunder. You can rant and rave to Austin and Jackson. They haven't heard your do-good speeches yet."

"Mom, you were the one lecturing." Darlene's thick eyebrows rose. "And since when did you start calling him Jackson instead of Mr. Armstrong?"

"This morning."

"Getting kind of personal, aren't ya? You hardly ever call anyone by their first name."

"He asked me to, baby. Don't get so worried. It doesn't mean anything."

Darlene moved her head away from Camille and watched the elk.

"Yeah," Camille said, gently grabbing her daughter's chin and pulling it around to face her. "Nothing is happening between us."

"I'm not worried about that."

"Then what is it?"

"You're going to get your heart broken again, and I don't know if I can handle it."

Camille sighed. "I'm not going to get my heart broken. I already told you he's not my type. Besides, if I did make such a mistake, I'm strong enough to survive quite nicely."

"Are you?" Darlene asked. "I see what this divorce thing did to you. Don't think because I'm not married I don't have eyes. I saw how it tore you up. You used to walk with confidence. Nothing got in your way. Now you run and hide because of a holiday. Do me a favor and please forget Jackson."

"I don't get it," Camille said. "You bugged me endlessly to be interested in Jackson yesterday. Now in less than twenty-four hours, you're practically begging me to stay away. What happened?"

Her daughter sat with her shoulder slumped forward, as if taking on the weight of the universe. "Mom, he's bad news. That's all I can say."

A honk forced their attention to Austin's truck. They were moving on.

"Oh, wait," Camille said. "I need to get a picture of this for my book."

They got out of the car and hiked through the brown weeds. Darlene held up one finger at the truck as Camille fumbled with her camera. Camille opted for getting a close-up of an elk eating, and also a picture of the whole herd. The elk she chose had massive antlers that spread across the back. "That rack is a work of art," she mumbled.

"They look heavy," Darlene said.

"Up to forty pounds." Camille changed her lens to snap the group picture.

"I like their white rumps."

"Darlene!" Camille struggled not to laugh. "I guess they do stand out."

"It's kind of hard to miss a white tail end when the rest of you is brown," Darlene said.

"The Shawnees thought so too. They named the elk 'wapiti.' It means 'white rump.'"

Darlene laughed. "That's great."

Camille waved to the men in the truck, signaling them to wait a bit longer. "Actually, the early colonists gave the names to the animals. Wapiti was their word for European moose."

"Those colonists sure did whatever they wanted," Darlene commented. "It's too bad we didn't see an elk fight or anything."

"It is," Camille agreed. "It's the rutting season. Did you know some of the more studly bulls have up to sixty cows in their harem?"

"Disgusting."

———

Jackson was watching the women hurry through the weeds when his son launched into him. "You should remember not to flirt with other women when you're still hoping to get back with Mom," Austin spat.

There was an undercurrent of anger and hurt in Austin's voice, but

Jackson couldn't help flaring up at such an accusation. "Who says I flirted? Your mom isn't filling you with hogwash, is she?"

"She doesn't have to when I have my own eyes."

"What are you talking about?"

"Don't play dumb with me. I've seen how you carry on with that Britain lady. It's gross."

Jackson pondered a minute. Had he flirted with Camille? He didn't think so. He sighed, long and heavy. But what if he had? He was divorced, after all. Poor Austin was glaring at him as if Jackson had been the one to walk out on the marriage. This was the typical I-want-my-parents-to-stay-together syndrome. The boy was still trying to build his fairytale. Jackson had thought his son was too old to go through that stage, but apparently not.

"I know it must be hard to see your parents separated," Jackson said, "but we have to go on. We have to live. We can't moan about what we lost the rest of our lives."

"You could get Mom back if you wanted."

"Think so?" Jackson said, breath gusting from him. Did Austin know something? Had Maggie realized her mistake and told Austin about it?

"Of course. I bet a counselor would have you guys fixed in no time. A month, tops."

Nope, Maggie hadn't confided anything to their child. It was simply Austin's adolescent dream that his family would be whole again. He eyed his son. He couldn't blame Austin for feeling that way because he, too, wished they were a whole family, but that wasn't reality. "It's not that simple, Austin."

"Yes it is. You belong with Mom."

"I'm sorry, kid. I really am. I'd like to be with your mother, but she won't have me, and you can't force people to do what they don't want to do."

"She talks about you a lot."

"All bad, I'm sure."

"She said you were the most handsome guy she ever laid eyes on when you first met."

"Too bad I got old," Jackson said.

"Dad, stop it."

"I can't talk about this anymore."

"Why?"

"Just can't."

———

The car halted next to the pale blue Yellowstone River, flowing northward in its rocky bed. Sagebrush and close-cropped grass mixed with a few towering pines, and gray mountains rested in the background. A few Canadian geese, pelicans, and ducks lingered in the water, preparing for migration to a warmer climate. Dull and rich greens contrasted with orange and mush brown. Again Camille remained speechless. She sat in the heart of Yellowstone. No wonder this area inspired Ferdinand Hayden to preserve its richness and form a national park.

Jackson tapped on the window, and Camille fumbled to open the door. "We need to hurry if we're going to see any bears." The intensity of his brown eyes bathed her with a thermal effect like the hot springs, but she showed no response as a courtesy to her daughter's over-active concern. Soon the group jogged down a dirt path, with Jackson in the lead. Wind pushed against them, bringing a chill. They stopped at a grassy clearing to set up.

"Why are we facing the river instead of the trees?" Darlene asked.

"Bears like to fish after feasting on pine nuts," Austin whispered.

"They'll go back to sleep at about ten or eleven." Jackson scanned the landscape with his spotting scope. "Ah, there's one." A huge brown bear lumbered forward on all fours, swatting at the river. Jackson and Austin hustled, preparing the equipment while the girls observed the magnificent beast. Muscles rippled through its back as the bear swung his enormous paw at an unseen fish.

"My editor's going to love this." Jackson changed locations and angles several times before the bear splashed through the water. Then Jackson unhooked the camera from the tripod and moved closer.

"This'll be awesome." The bear plowed into the river, not hearing the distant clicks. Cloud cover broke, and rays of warmth flowed onto the group.

"It's cold for a swim," Darlene said.

"It's about fifty-five degrees. Not too bad," Austin said. "I could live here forever."

"Why don't you?" Darlene asked.

"Told ya. Need to be a lawyer."

"Law's boring."

"I'll be perfectly happy as a lawyer, and I'll own the perfect cabin to stay in for half the perfect week, every week. It'll be perfectly great."

"I doubt you'd get many clients from around here," Camille said.

"A private jet fixes that."

Darlene shook her head, and when Austin walked over to his father, she said, "He won't be happy."

"Why the sudden interest?" Camille asked.

Startled, Darlene said, "I care about people."

"Uh-huh."

"It's true."

"Uh-huh."

"What? I don't like him," Darlene said. "I mean, I like him like I do everyone else, but I don't have a special interest in him."

"Sure."

"I don't!"

"Sorry, darling, I have eyes. Even a blind person could see how you light up when he's around."

"I don't—"

"There's nothing wrong with it." Camille almost couldn't believe she was saying that. It was as if the change in her opinion of Jackson somehow extended to his son as well.

"It's not true. I'm not interested in anyone who cares more about money and big houses than love and commitment. Besides, he's weird." She swiped at some hair that had blown across her eyes.

"How's that?"

"He's hard to get along with."

"Well, you two do have a lot in common."

"Like what?" Darlene picked a weed to twist in her hand.

"You both seem uneasy when Jackson and I are together."

"True, both of you are on the rebound. It's dangerous."

"What makes you think either one of us is interested?"

"Hah! Even a blind person could sense the sparks between you."

Camille laughed, brushing the comment aside, but it didn't go away easily. Could there be some truth there?

———

Jackson concentrated on taking inventory of what would be in his picture: the bear, splashing water, purple mountains, and the ducks flying into the horizon. Perfect. His editor would throw in a bonus. Why had he stayed behind the desk for so long? Maybe Maggie had done a good thing for him when she'd left. Now if he could just arrange for her to find him in the company of Camille. That would be perfect.

Camille possessed self-confidence, charm, and a natural beauty that would ignite a spark of jealousy in Maggie. And meanwhile, Camille was fun to be around now that she'd loosened up a bit. A huge flash of guilt overcame Jackson. Camille was too nice a lady to use. Was that what he was doing?

Austin walked up to him. "Did you get the picture?"

Jackson nodded, spotting Camille and Darlene hiking up the slope.

"Dad!" Austin whispered.

"What?"

"Let's dump the girls. We could suggest going on a fifteen-mile hike, and I bet they'd wimp out."

"You underestimate Darlene. She's a trooper."

"She's a pain. She's always bossing me around. She won't listen to an ounce of logic."

"Better get used to it, boy." Jackson patted his son's shoulder. "All women are like that."

"But Dad, let's get away from—"

Jackson hastened his pace to catch up to the ladies. "I got the best shots," he called out. "I'll develop them tonight and mail them to my editor. He's going to be excited, especially with the bear running through the water. I can't wait to see how they turned out."

"Mail them?" Darlene looked shocked. "I thought everyone used digital these days."

Jackson smiled. "I actually use both, but I prefer the old method." He took big strides up the mountain, and the women fell in behind. "Let's go to Old Faithful for lunch," he said.

"But what about visiting Cody?" Darlene asked.

"Ah, yes. There's too much to do in one day. I say we make several trips here and plan them better so we can see more of the sights."

"Sounds great," Camille responded. Then smiling up at Jackson, she asked, "Would you mind helping with the research for my book and class? You seem to know a lot about this place. With your input, and Austin's, I could make this a really interactive and useful course. I promised my bosses I'd teach important issues about the environment and animal habitat."

"There's a crusade both Austin and I would be glad to join. We're a bit of environmentalists ourselves. Aren't we, Austin?"

His son grunted.

Jackson offered his hand to pull Camille up the last of the incline. "Tell you what, little lady, why don't you choose where we go for lunch, since it's your research?"

"Please don't call me little lady," Camille protested, though his offer was thoughtful. "Well, I really need to hit some stores to find hands-on material. I was planning a whole section on the geysers, hot springs, hot pools, and fumaroles. The more information I collect, and the more I see, the better off I'll be."

"Sounds like Old Faithful country to me. Come on, troops. Darlene, why don't you go with Austin so I can tell your mom the information she needs? I'm sure the more work she gets done the better she'll feel, especially since the park will be closing in a couple of weeks."

"Closing!" Camille said.

"Yeah. The roads will be covered with snow, and the only way in or out will be by snowmobile. We can plan one of those trips when you have most of your work done. I promised my editor a whole bunch of winter scenes."

"I didn't know the park closed." Desperation filled Camille. She really needed to get busy. She waved to Darlene and Austin. "See you two at Old Faithful."

"Actually we'll be stopping at a couple places along the way," Jackson said. "You won't want to miss the West Thumb Geyser Basin."

Camille saluted. "You heard what the boss said."

Once on their way, Camille and Jackson became heavily involved in planning her course. She watched his beard-shadowed face as he talked and drove. A surprisingly helpful man.

"It's surprising—you sure know a lot for being a . . ." her voice trailed off because she wasn't able to think of an inoffensive word for hick.

"Being a what?" Jackson asked.

"I don't know."

"Yes, you do."

Camille sighed. "You have this annoying habit of persistence."

"Isn't that great? I didn't ask such a difficult question, did I?"

"I'm sorry. Your question led to reflection."

"Tell me."

"I shouldn't."

"Do."

She put down the pen. "I really don't want you to take it wrong."

"Give me a try."

"It's nice that you're dependable. I'm learning that I can count on you wanting to know everything, good or bad."

His face reddened. "You're saying that I'm predictable."

"Oh, no, no." Her hand rested on his arm as if to comfort him. "Don't get me wrong. You have very fine qualities. I can't understand why your ex-wife would use 'predictability' as a reason for divorce. I find dependability comforting. A person knows where they stand. I know if I make a mistake and don't finish my statement, you're going to jump on my case and pester me until I do. When I was with my husband, he always changed the rules. If I didn't finish my sentence one day, he wouldn't notice. The next he'd laugh at my inability to think before I spoke, and the following day he'd be angry at my lack of consideration for his time. I bet if I were a baseball player and you were the pitcher and I went to bat, a thousand times you'd throw a strike. You're consistent. You'd always make me finish my sentence. Am I right?"

"Yep." His eyes seemed to light up. "Every single time, like I'm going to do now. You went on a great verbal excursion. I have to give you credit for that. Now tell me what you were going to say?"

"I forgot."

"That's a good one." Jackson winked. "I'll play along with your game this once. You said I knew a lot for being a . . . Please fill in the blank and be honest."

"I dug myself in deep this time." She shook her head. "I'll have to learn to keep my mouth shut."

"Out with it."

"I'm going to prove myself the educated snob you accused me of being. I was going to say you knew a lot for being a hick."

"Hick? Is that what you think?"

"Well, you do live in the mountains, and your English isn't always proper, and you like to hunt, and frankly, you don't seem to have any city in you. You appear to belong here, and it seems that cars, people, and stores would be a hindrance to your happiness."

Jackson drove in silence, not responding to her observations. She'd probably offended him.

"Well?" she pressed.

"I see."

"Aren't you going to say anything else?"

"Nope."

"You're not going to prove me wrong or zap me with a comment on my hypocrisy?"

"Nope. You might have snobby outlooks, but at least you're honest. That's more than I can say for a lot of people."

"I'm glad you find it refreshing," she mumbled, feeling as if there had been a seven point six earthquake and she'd fallen into a newly made crack. Every time she tried to do anything, the earth shifted and she sunk in deeper.

"Do you like your photography job now?" she ventured.

"Yes. It's different than anything I've ever done. At times, when it's cold and I'm dead tired, I think about a more comfortable job. But then I remember all this beauty."

"So you think your divorce was a positive thing in your life?" Camille asked.

"I don't know if I'd say that. Divorce is painful and horrible. I wouldn't wish it on anyone, but I also believe we have to make the best of what happens."

"My oldest boy thinks I'm running from my problems by coming out here," Camille said.

"Are you?"

"Hard to say. Are you?"

Jackson laughed. "No, just getting on with my life and doing some things I dreamed about but was too tied down to do. And of course, living my life as a hick."

"I bet I'll never hear the end of that comment."

Jackson just smiled.

———

Darlene slammed the truck door. Austin didn't look at her as his stomach tightened. "You're doing a lousy job keeping them apart," he said. "My dad won't listen to me because your mom's so busy distracting him."

"It's your father who is leading her on," Darlene snapped. A thin line of red marred her skin at the top of her cheekbones.

"He's not." Austin steered the car onto the blacktop.

"Then exactly what do you call it? According to you, he plans to get back with your mom."

"It's your mom who's flirting, acting all interested in his job and sneaking him *those* looks."

"That's not flirting. That's conversation. Hasn't anyone ever flirted with you?"

Austin straightened his shoulders. "Tons of girls."

Darlene rolled her eyes. "Then you should know what flirting is. Girls don't do what you say. They stare long and hard and wait for the guy to glance back. When he does, they act embarrassed and get this stupid grin, then they sneak a sly glimpse when they know they have the guy's attention. They also run up to him, touch him and laugh this silly high-pitched giggle, and bat their eyes. *That's* flirting."

"There's more than one way to flirt. Your mother likes my father. She's making it clear through internal waves."

"Internal what?"

"Internal waves." He waved his hand like it was one of those jagged lines on a heart monitor. "You know. You send messages to others by not saying anything. Body language."

"Like how?" Darlene asked.

"I haven't studied enough to say exactly," he said, rubbing the dark stubble on his chin, "but she's communicating it."

"You have no proof," Darlene said.

"I'll get evidence."

"I already have evidence that your father is guilty." Darlene wore an amused smile. Her delicate features gave the feeling of a strong determination underneath.

"What?" He watched her determined facial expression become even more solid.

"He ran off to take a picture of the bear down the slope, didn't he?"

"Yeah."

"When he came back, didn't he jog to my mom and me?"

"That doesn't—"

"Who did he come up to? Me or my mother?"

"That's just—"

"Me or my mother?"

"Your mother. But that's just circumstantial."

"Okay then. What crafty person arranged for our parents to drive together?" Darlene paused, enjoying the moment before the trap sprung down. "Your father. Your sneaky, lying father, who's preying on a vulnerable woman."

"Just a minute," he said. "Your mother isn't perfect. She did give him several seductive smiles, luring him on."

"Did not." Her voice rose.

"My father isn't the jerk you make him out to be."

"I didn't say he was."

"Did."

"I said he was that way with my mother. I didn't say with *every* female."

He drummed his fingers on the steering wheel, breathing deeply before this got really nasty. "This is getting us nowhere."

The statement seemed to calm Darlene enough that she didn't say any more. She looked out the window. Austin continued to drive as his heart thumped hard against his chest. Neither one of them liked being stuck together. Silence was the best thing. And that was the way it stayed until Darlene broke out into a loud laugh.

"What's so funny?" Austin snapped.

"It dawned on me that we're playing out the living version of Romeo and Juliet."

"What?"

"It's role reversal. Our parents could be falling in love with each other and *we're* the ones feuding."

"So they're going to kill themselves because we're denying them a relationship?" he asked.

"No. We're worried about them getting hurt. I know my mom isn't thinking clearly and will be devastated if your father doesn't put an end to this."

"But—"

"But like Romeo and Juliet, the more we try to push them away, the closer they'll get."

"Maybe."

Darlene smiled. "Thanks for admitting to my brilliance."

"So, Miss Brilliant One, what are we going to do?"

"What's your idea?"

"I don't have one."

Darlene flung a strand of hair off her shoulder. "So, we're back to square one. Let's forget about our parents for a while." She switched the radio to a twangy song. A man singing about drinking and wishing his lady was still in his life. "I want to know more about the Yellowstone classes. Can I take one while I'm here?" Darlene yelled over the song.

Austin turned down the volume. "You could take several and get credits. Are you in college?"

"I was supposed to start this term. But I don't know." She shifted in her seat.

"Why not? Hate studying?"

"I hate being told what to do and when to do it, and then tested on what the teacher thinks is important. They miss the boat a lot."

"But you have to pay the price to get the degree—a passport to go places in this world. That's the rules."

"I hate rules."

"So does my mom."

"What's she like?"

The song stopped and a string of commercials came on. Austin paused to give the question due respect. Finally he spoke up in the middle of a car advertisement. "Gorgeous. I mean, drop dead stunning. She used to be a model but gave it up for me."

"Wow!"

"Tell you the truth, I don't know how she ever did it. Not that she couldn't smile and pose. I'm sure she was great at that, but the idea of my mom following a schedule? I still can't see it. She never stuck to anything for more than two days, and she never keeps her appointments." He glanced at her, a half-cocked smile on his face. "You remind me of her. She hated rules. Santa came two weeks early or two weeks late, but never on Christmas day because she hated celebrating a holiday on the day the calendar said. Sometimes my mom would come and wake me up at three in the morning, saying it was lunch time."

"I'm not that bad. I'd hate that," Darlene said.

"What could I do?"

"Go back to sleep."

Austin laughed. "There's no ignoring my mom. Even if you tried, you couldn't."

"Sounds interesting."

"She is. The best kind to have around. Life's dull when she's gone. What's your father like?"

"My father?"

"I told you about my mom. It's only fair."

"He's charming," Darlene said. "If I managed to pull him away from the computer, he told funny stories about his work. He'd be funny, but in a serious way—like he never knew he was being funny. And he wasn't happy that I'd stolen him away from his work. You could always tell he was bugged if he wasn't working. He's one of those geeks who plays with his computer for hours to figure out the different things it can do."

"What kind of work does he do?"

"I don't know. Something with stocks and bonds."

"Do you have a brother or sister?"

"Older brother. He's married now, with a kid. How about you? Any siblings to torture your existence?"

"None."

"Ah, that explains it."

"What?" He looked at the playful expression she wore so innocently. She brushed at a strand of her long hair before saying, "The fact that you're spoiled."

"Am not."

"If you say so," she said.

Austin rolled his eyes. "You really like to get under my skin." She broke into a fantastic smile, which made it so he couldn't keep from smiling back, amused at her poke. "I have to admit you're fun," he added.

"Yeah, you too."

"Anything for you, babe," Austin said with his eyebrows going up and down.

She laughed. "It looks like you have some of your mom in you."

"A speck of both parents and a little of just me."

"You've really gotten me curious about your mom. I'd like to meet her someday."

"You will. She promised she'd come. That's when Dad will fix things between them. If I know him, he's already got a plan."

The time passed quickly. Soon the group stopped and left the cars to see the sights. Austin looked over the landscape at the looming blue mountains, the white puffy clouds topping them, and the hot springs like scattered paint pots bubbling and steaming in a polka dot pattern on the ground. West Thumb Geyser Basin.

"I got the challenge," he said, talking behind Darlene's shoulder.

"What?" She turned to face him.

"The new challenge. What you have to do is see how close to the edge of the wooden bridge you can walk."

"You mean," her voice cracked, "the bridge over there leading above the boiling pots?"

"Exactly."

"What happens if you fall in?"

"People die every year doing that."

Darlene stared at him, and he felt smug with victory. He didn't think she had the nerve to do something like that. Her next words surprised him. "You're on."

They raced through the parking lot, and then onto the wooden bridge, the crosswalk bouncing under the weight of their steps. Austin pulled ahead and made it over the guardrail. He balanced himself on the thin ledge of wood, and Darlene followed. Over her head, he could see her mom charging toward them. She looked like a panicked bird whose young was about to be eaten.

"No fair holding onto the handrail," Darlene said at the same time her mom screeched. Austin let go of the handrail, holding his hands high above him.

"Get back over that fence this instant!" Camille snapped, pointing to the center of the crosswalk.

"Got a bet with Darlene," Austin said.

"I don't care if you have a pact with the devil himself," Jackson said, appearing around Camille. "If you don't get onto the right side now, I'm repossessing your truck."

Austin reluctantly climbed back over.

Camille grabbed Darlene's wrist before she could give it a try. "Don't even think about it."

———

That attempt from the young adults put a damper on everyone's good mood. The group didn't stay long at the site. They were back into their vehicles when Camille noticed the stiff way Jackson carried himself. It was as if a cloud of unrest had wrapped around him, pressing in on him.

"Are you okay?" She touched his forearm.

"I don't want to talk about it," he said, getting into the car. They drove past several signs before Jackson said, "I'm sorry. I didn't mean to be rude. I was caught off guard."

"No, you were fine. I understand completely. I've had my times, too." She wondered if she should push the conversation. Would he want to talk or would he resist her intrusion? "Sometimes it helps to talk. Maybe get an objective perceptive. I know my daughter was about to do it too, but I don't think—"

"It wasn't what they did," Jackson broke in. "It's what it reminded me of."

"Do you mind if I asked what that is?" She waited, saw the muscles in his square, stubbled face flinch. "Sorry. I shouldn't have asked." Her voice lowered as she glanced at the sky. Clouds had started to spread over the blueness.

"No, you were fine. I'm sorry. I'm normally not like this. I'm caught up in a memory and I can't shake it."

Camille stayed silent, hearing the pain in his voice.

"When I was young," Jackson continued, "I wouldn't listen to anyone, just like Austin. It hurts to realize how much of my foolishness he inherited. Stubborn one, that boy is. Very stubborn."

"Also like his father?" Camille ventured to ask.

He turned his head so fast to look at her, Camille thought for sure she had said the wrong thing. She waited for his rebuke, but he surprised her by smiling. "Yeah, like his dad in both the foolishness and being stubborn. You hate to see your kids picking up the same problems you have. I hope Austin can avoid some of the pain I went through."

"I feel the same way about my kids."

Jackson seemed to like that connection, as though it gave him what he needed to open up.

"I used to take swims in the canal. One day my mom said I couldn't because it was Friday the Thirteenth. She was superstitious. Thinking that was stupid, I waited until my mom was out of hearing distance and challenged my brother to a race. He didn't want to get in trouble. I called him a chicken, flapping my arms like wings and everything. He tried to defend himself, but I wouldn't listen and took off running toward the canal. He followed, yelling that I cheated. When we got to the canal, we both jumped in, laughing and arguing about who had actually cheated. Then I got this bright idea to race across the river."

He took a deep breath and Camille felt trepidation, suspecting the story didn't end well.

After a long pause, Jackson continued, "My brother was possessed. He had to beat me, but I couldn't let him show me up, so I swam faster and faster. When I made it to the other side, I looked around to see how far behind he was, but I couldn't see him." He swallowed once and then again. "The officials discover his body three days later. They said he'd been caught in an undercurrent and . . . and drowned."

"No!" Camille gasped.

"I killed my little brother."

Camille gazed into his eyes that were so much like a vulnerable child's, wishing she could take away his pain.

CHAPTER EIGHT

The last rays of sunlight shot through the graying sky. A few passing cars turned on their headlights, beams not yet cutting through the darkness. Camille and Jackson had driven behind their kids for over an hour, their conversation drifting into silence, leaving only the dog panting around the bed of Austin's pick-up truck. It wasn't until the dog began a round of insistent barking that Camille gripped her seatbelt, mumbling.

"Beg your pardon?" Jackson turned to her.

"Your dog's yapping. That's supposed to be a sign there's an evil spirit around." The car lights hit the rustling vegetation.

"Nonsense."

"Maybe." Camille drew her lips tight. "They say a dog howling at night is a sure sign."

"I don't buy that superstition stuff."

"I really don't believe most of it either, but, honestly, this one has never failed."

"Care to place a bet on it?"

"I'll put my money where my mouth is," she said.

"Okay. I'll bet you another date to Yellowstone. If I win, you'll agree to go on the trip with me."

"And if I win?"

"You can have my service as Mr. Fix-It for anything you choose," Jackson said.

"What makes you think I'll need your services?"

"Do you want to take that question back?" There was a hint of laughter in his voice.

"Generous, aren't we?"

"I try to be a gentleman when I can."

"If that's the case, then you've got yourself a wager. And don't think I won't be staying up all night planning what you can help me with. That's exactly what I'll be doing."

"Whatever. Let's set a time limit to make the deal concrete."

"Fine. Two weeks."

He laughed. "Two days at most."

"Okay, if in five days an evil person doesn't make itself known, then you win." Jackson shook her hand. She noticed the strength of his grip.

"When did you learn to bargain?" he asked.

"One of my many skills."

"I'm sure."

Jackson was still thinking about their odd bet after dropping Camille off. When he arrived at his own cabin, Austin jumped from his truck and ran up to him. "I'm glad that's over. I think."

Jackson smiled. He knew he should be relieved to have time for his own thoughts, but if he told the truth, he was anticipating the next chance he would have to see Camille. "It was a fun day."

"Yeah, but that lady's a bit weird, isn't she?"

"Well, Camille sure is a different breed." He wouldn't exactly say weird.

"Yeah, and the nut doesn't fall too far from the tree."

Jackson laughed. "You're saying Darlene's odd too?"

"Oh, yeah!"

Jackson hurried into the house and found four messages awaiting him. He picked up the phone so Austin wouldn't hear. Beep. "Hey, Jaxy, call me now." Beep. "Jackson, I need to talk to you,

ASAP." Beep. Click. Beep. "Jackson, call me. This has to do with your son."

The muscles in Jackson's chest tightened. What was she up to? That woman was capable of making his life miserable if he upset her too much, and he didn't think divorce would have changed that. He needed to call Maggie. Now, before she became more uptight. She didn't sound happy about waiting. His breath grew heavy as he dialed. The phone rang in slow, seemingly drawn out time. The phone rang one, two . . . five times. Finally, after six long rings, the answering machine said, "Hello, you've reached Maggie Armstrong. Leave me a message and I'll get right back to you."

He left the message that he was returning her call and would try again.

———

Camille collapsed on her bed, not wanting to move. The day had been a welcome change from Halloween, and Jackson had proved to be a wonderful help in outlining her course and book. Maybe she'd give him credit on the front page. Tomorrow promised to be quiet and restful, with maybe some sightseeing. Perhaps luck would be with them and she'd find an arrowhead. Not that she needed one—she'd already bought several at the Old Faithful store—but to find one on her own would give her work an added sense of authenticity.

The bedroom door creaked, and in tiptoed Darlene. "Good night, Mom." She slipped over to the bed and gave her mom a peck on the cheek.

Camille kissed her daughter goodnight and soon fell asleep. She was not disturbed again until sunlight sparkled through the drapes. She rose and gazed out her window. Island Park was a completely different place in the early fall morning—more heavenly. It was as if a painter had dabbed his brush in a calming pale blue with a touch of gray and spread the color over the sky, air, and water. Next, the artist took grayish-white oil and painted fog rising off the water and white clouds fading in the background. The artist wouldn't be able to paint the clean, chilled air, but he would add the finishing touches of fog clinging to the surrounding vegetation.

They were getting ready for their trip down the Reservoir when Jackson and Austin appeared. "Hey, I was wondering if you'd like to go to Big Springs with us to feed the fish," Jackson said. "It's sort of a tradition around here on Sundays."

Not being one to break tradition, Camille agreed. "Sure." She almost expected Darlene to protest, but she and Austin were deep in their own private discussion, looking happy to see each other.

During the drive, the scenery changed little. Tall, thin pine trees were everywhere, and the Tetons sat majestically in the distance against a pale blue sky. When they arrived, Camille could see two wooden bridges crossed the Snake River at Big Springs. She was surprised at how shallow and crystal clear the water was, and she couldn't believe the rich golds and blues of the rainbow trout. Pieces of bread floated by the fish. Amphibians bit some crumbs and ignored others. The water gurgled around the stones in the stream, forming a current. All this, and the fresh, pine-scented air as well. Camille climbed on the bottom pole of the bridge's handrail to get a better glimpse of the fish, smelling Jackson's pleasant cologne before he spoke a word.

"Beautiful, aren't they?" he asked as he handed her a piece of bread. "The forest rangers protect them. Fishing isn't allowed." Seating himself on the handrail, he changed his tone by asking, "See any evil spirits?"

She eyed the crowd around them. "Lots of suspects."

"Suspects for what?" Austin questioned, joining them.

"Evil spirits." Jackson winked at Camille.

Darlene approached the group. She had been collecting wild-flowers and slipped some yellow and pink flowers in her hair. She hovered close to Camille and tugged on her shirt sleeve. "Hey, Mom. Let's go. I'm getting hungry."

"But you gotta see John Sack's cabin." Jackson pointed to a log home nestled into the hillside.

"Ohhh!" Camille said. "A historical site."

"It's just a stupid cabin," Austin said.

"The hike's short." Jackson tapped his son on the shoulder.

"I'd love to see it. It looks like it was built in the early nineteen hundreds," Camille said.

"Good eye." Jackson herded the group toward the path. "John Sack was famous for his craftsmanship. He designed rustic furniture from conifers. Inside the cabin, the logs still have bark on them. That's not something you see often."

"You sound like a history buff." Camille fell in line behind him.

"Carpentry interests me. The bark logs are incredible because they have been cut to fit exactly. You can see the white wood under the brown bark."

"Artsy," Camille said.

"It is."

The hike to Sack's cabin had a rejuvenating effect on Camille. Her eyes feasted on the idyllic scenery that looked like it originated straight out of a Thomas Kinkade painting. A brilliant display of color harmonized throughout, from the rich earthy tones in the rocks that formed a path across the sparkling creek to the ivory clouds compressed over the purple-blue sky, the jagged mountains, and the thick forest of vegetation. When the group made it to the cabin, Camille was convinced this home had captured paradise.

Soon they joined a group of other tourists, listening to the tour guide give his spiel. One of the first rooms they came to was the guest quarters with an old-fashioned bed and quilt for a bedspread. "Did John have a wife and kids?" Camille asked, hoping to hear that John Sack had captured a dream life, giving her hope that someday she'd find the peace and fulfillment she longed for.

"No. He was interested in a young lady named Estelle, but she married Harry Phillips. He was the founder of Phillips' Lodge."

"How sad. To live in all this beauty and not be able to share it with someone," Camille heard Darlene say.

Camille peered around the tourists to catch a glimpse of her daughter. Instead, her eyes connected with Jackson, who towered in the back above the rest. The same electric volt shot through her as yesterday on the Yellowstone trip. A flush of understanding came from him then and now. She had the unnerving impression that he could read her thoughts or at least know about her search for completeness. His eyes said that even though Mr. Sack hadn't achieved completeness, that didn't mean she couldn't.

The tour guide broke into their eye exchange by leading the group into the next room. Embarrassed, Camille avoided Jackson's eyes throughout the rest of the tour and during the hike back. Before the group reached the cars, Darlene started into her normal complaints. "I'm so hungry. It's going to be *forever* until we get something made." On and on she whined.

Barely listening, Camille wondered why her heart beat so hard. Could it be from the hike? Her heart rate increased further when Jackson said to Darlene, "Why don't you and your pretty mom come over to my place? I'll fix the best grilled chicken sandwiches you've ever tasted."

Camille tried to ignore the word "pretty" and the renewed wash of heat on her face as she said, "We could stop by my cabin first and grab ice cream. It'd make it a feast."

"Deal."

Camille went faint in the knees. What was Jackson thinking when he looked at her like that? Perhaps acting like an authentic family for a Sunday was like a nibble of normalcy, the ideal family they'd both lost since the breakup of their marriages. Filling the void for a day was a relief, a taste of heaven. Of course, she couldn't forget this was just a substitute. She still craved to have the real thing with real love, not just go through the motions. Maybe he had similar feelings.

Camille looked at the growing trees as they drove past. They had suffered a beetle infestation in the 1980's. It had nearly wiped out the area. In an effort to recover, the forest rangers and locals actively worked at planting more trees to replace the loss. Someone had posted brown signs with yellow numbers painted on them, signaling when this batch or that stand of new trees had been planted. The land was starting anew, just as she and Jackson were.

She continued to gaze at the trees until a solitary black bird swooped down through the sky, catching her attention. The bird shot high in the air and then dove downward like a descending missile, landing on the telephone wire. There it perched as though it were a sentry. Camille couldn't help but be amused. A bird landing in front of a person was a sign of an approaching enemy—so perhaps she would win the bet with Jackson after all. She'd better start thinking about the fix-it jobs she could have him do.

By the time they pulled up to the reservoir, the sun had risen high enough to cast a golden glow on the flourishing life of birds, fish, and a multitude of creatures stirring in the surrounding forest. A satisfying contentment settled in Camille's heart.

At Jackson's cabin, he and Camille set to work preparing lunch. They talked about their favorite dishes as Darlene sulked at the kitchen counter. Austin hung farther away, hands in front pockets, his face showing no emotion.

Camille didn't comment on their children's obvious dismay, nor did she show any hint that she knew they were around. If she ignored their attitudes, it would do one of two things: either make the children's pouting dissolve from lack of attention or escalate their disapproval. Either way, she didn't have to worry about it for now.

Hardly a word was spoken during the meal until Camille said, "This chicken is great, Jackson. You can cook for me any day."

"I'm at your service," Jackson said with a nod.

"Gag." Darlene stood to take her dish to the sink.

"Double gag," Austin said, following behind.

"Looks like we're being typical parents," Camille said. "Our young adults don't approve of us."

"That's right. We don't," Darlene said.

"Then I guess you don't approve of having ice cream," Camille countered.

"I wouldn't take it that far," Austin said, pulling the two containers of chocolate from the freezer.

After they devoured the dessert, the group sank lazily into chairs or onto couches in the red and blue family room near the back of the house. Camille studied the masculine cowboy decor and must have fallen asleep when an angry exclamation erupted in the room, snapping her to attention, dazed and confused.

It took her a while to realize where she was and that Jackson was staring out the back window, turned away from her. The exclamation had apparently come from him. She sat up to get a better glimpse of what he was seeing. Her movement seemed to startle Jackson, and he jerked around, looking almost surprised to see her sitting there watching him, but he quickly recovered. "I'm sorry. This might be awkward. I promise, though, it will definitely be a show."

"Wh—?" was all she choked out before her words were chased away by the sight of a stunning, china doll lady standing on the deck. The woman was a man's version of perfection—curves, flawless skin, silky hair, and confidence.

"Where are you going, Dad?" Austin mumbled sleepily from the couch. Then he jumped up, rushed to the door and threw it open. "Mom!"

Camille walked over to Jackson, who offered his arm to her. Surprised at the gesture, she accepted. Then she knew why he had offered his arm: for her to support him. He was shaking. She grasped his arm more firmly. The tightness of his muscles steadied her, and she gave him a wide smile. She whispered, "Jackson, going anywhere with you is an adventure. I admire your free spirit."

He reached over with his other hand and patted hers.

"What's the meaning of this?" the blonde asked.

"Good morning, Maggie," Jackson said. "Or should I say afternoon?"

"Who's your friend?"

"Maggie Campbell, this is Camille Britain. She's a history professor who's come to Island Park to research a book. Her daughter is the one over in that chair sleeping."

"Isn't that nice?" Maggie said with calculated sweetness. Her eyes scanned over Camille before brushing her hair behind her ear. "You do look like the intellectual type." Swiftly, she turned to Jackson and said, "It's been a long time since we've seen each other."

"Two months," he said. Camille let go of his arm, watching the performance.

"It seems like an eternity." Maggie rolled her words together, giving the impression of sweet honey—sweet, poisoned honey. "You've changed," she added, her eyes studying him. She smiled. "For the better—tan and trim."

"Glad you think so," Jackson said. "If you'll excuse me, Camille and I are heading off on our walk. We better get going." He nudged her forward.

"Don't play games," Maggie said. "You're just saying that to make me jealous."

Jackson flushed and Camille wondered if that was the truth. Maybe Jackson wanted his wife back. How could he not? She was so beautiful. "Why don't you two take a walk?" Camille asked.

"I don't want to go on a walk. Look, I don't have time for all this, Jackson. It is very important that I talk to you right now." Maggie raised a delicately arched brow on her perfectly shaped face. She was the type of woman men fell head-over-heels for. The type of woman men rushed to help. The type of woman Camille disliked because they relied on skills of manipulation instead of on themselves.

"Buuuttt," Jackson said. He seemed so flustered he couldn't manage to get another word out.

Camille patted him on the arm. "Go ahead and talk to her."

"I'm sorry about this," he said. "Why don't you let Austin take my place on the walk? Austin, would you mind? Darlene can join you too." Darlene had awakened and was standing in the background with a puzzled expression on her face.

Austin strolled to Camille and offered his arm. "Not at all. This way, madam." As he passed his mom, he stopped. Maggie grabbed his face between her hands and kissed him on both cheeks. Austin gave a happy laugh and a glance at Darlene that said something Camille didn't understand.

When Camille and the kids reached the main road, Darlene laughed, pointing her finger at Austin. "She drowned you in lipstick. Looks like you cut yourself shaving."

"Shut up." Austin wiped his cheeks.

Darlene laughed even harder. "Red's a good color on you."

"I mean it. You're going to get it if you don't stop."

"Get what?" Darlene challenged.

"Get poked with thistles." He dashed to a clump of purple flowers.

Darlene screamed and ran away. Austin ran after her, but he didn't take the flowers. By the time Camille caught up to them, they were talking companionably.

They continued through the mid-day heat, following the circling dirt road around the island. The light chatter of her daughter and her young adult male companion sounded far away, even though they were only a few steps in front of Camille. It was as if a vacuum sucked away the words, leaving a faint muddle of noise trailing behind them. On top of their static, Camille could hear in her mind the low, sensual voice of Maggie as she spoke the name "Jackson." The inflection she used had a possessive, demanding quality that could drive a person mad.

Camille couldn't shake the chime of Maggie's voice or her flawless skin, Barbie-doll figure, and devious eyes. *None of that matters,* Camille thought, feeling herself sink into a deep, wallowing pool of depression. But it seemed impossible for a man not to be completely lured into the charmed charismatic spell Maggie cast. She was Jackson's ex-wife and Austin's mother. She had every right to be there. It was Camille who was misplaced, and it was Camille who was the stranger, the interloper.

The group hadn't gone far when Camille made an excuse of feeling tired. "I'm heading home."

"I'll drive you if you like, Miss Britain," Austin said.

Miss. That's what she was now. "Thank you, but I'd rather walk."

"Wait up, Mom. I'm coming." Darlene hurried toward her.

"Stay and have some fun."

"But—" Camille heard Darlene say before she strode away.

Camille had to pass Jackson's cabin on the way. The sun was hidden as the wind puffed in graying skies, dotted with clouds. The rugged deep blues, purples, and greens of the mountains stood jagged behind the water. The reservoir was deep gray near Jackson's cabin, and the couple who stood in front of the water were dark shadows.

What did it matter to her that Jackson talked to his wife? It was a natural thing. Why did it make her feel so awful?

———

Jackson stopped, staring at Maggie's sea-green eyes and silky, white skin as they strolled the beach. She'd trimmed her hair, allowing romantic tendrils to wrap around her face. She'd lost weight as well. "I called you," he said. "Did you get my message?"

"I miss you, Jaxy." She rolled his name around on her tongue as she reached out and touched his biceps. A shiver shot through him. The wind swept her short curls onto her face. She brushed her hair back then stood on her tiptoes and kissed him longingly. The roll of waves splashed near their feet. Jackson stood there, staring, stunned.

"I love you," Maggie whispered. "I love you."

"But I—I thought—" Jackson stammered. He'd dreamed of this happening. Of her seeing him with Camille and understanding how much she'd lost. Yet now that his dream might be coming true, he found he didn't trust it. Or her.

"We need to spend more time together. Look, I have to go in a couple minutes. I just barely had enough time to run up here and see you, but I'll be back soon."

The curve of her body and her flashy, demanding personality preyed on his longing. He kept his gaze on the dark reservoir. The water ruffled in the breeze, rolling its thick black waves in a whimsical fashion. His mind spun. It was as if Maggie stood right before him talking, touching him, yet he was suddenly miles away. He wanted to know what she said, but somehow, he couldn't focus. Now she was snuggling against his chest, kissing him lightly. She'd asked him a question. "Whaaat?" he asked.

She laughed. "I was just curious as to why you were hanging out with someone like that woman. She's hardly your type."

"Maggie, why are you really here?" he whispered.

111

"What, can't I come and visit, or is that not allowed?"

"It's allowed." He could see his fast response, his anxiousness, had registered its meaning to Maggie. She smiled, the kind of smile that leaped inside him. He wrapped his arms around her slender body. In a swiping motion, he bent to find her lips as he had done so many times before, but this time with anxious speed. When she pulled away from him, his heart hurt from the rapid beating. This was really happening.

The sinking sun highlighted the richness of her hair. He stroked it, gently pressing her head to rest against his chest. Her silky tresses brushed against his chin with a floral scent. But all too quickly, she pushed away, slipped her long, slender fingers around his large ones, and guided him back to the cabin. He didn't dare allow himself to think what this woman was up to.

She grabbed his forearm with a firm grip and pulled him to a stop halfway to the cabin. "I need you to do me a little favor."

"What's that?"

"I need you to spot me some cash."

"What? Why? I left you with plenty in the divorce."

Her thin index reached his lips as she whispered, "Shhh. Don't say such an ugly word."

"What's this about? Are we divorced or not?"

"It's not about that at all. I told you I don't want to talk about it. I can't deal with all that right now. I need time. I am in a bind. Can you help me out?" A boat in the lake zoomed past them, the headlights shining in the dying sunlight. Kids squealed in the back of the boat.

"How did you get in debt? I gave you more than plenty. I don't understand."

"I know. I'll explain it all later. We need to go inside. I haven't seen Austin in a long time, and he should be back from his stroll. This loan will benefit you a lot. It won't be very long before I make it up to you, double. I promise."

He took her clenched hands off his sleeves and squeezed them. "What have you gotten yourself into?"

"It's wonderful. Guaranteed. This is the best."

"Maggie."

"Will you please give me some money to tide me over?"

"Maggie."

She pulled him close and kissed him. Not a few-seconds smooch, but a long and passionate kiss. Her fingers slid through his hair as she pulled his head closer. After a long moment, she yanked back for a gasp of air. "Please, Jaxy, I'll pay you back. Promise."

He kissed her again. "Okay. I can't see how it would hurt."

She smiled as she held his hand. They walked through the hip-high weeds back to the cabin.

Austin pounced on them at the door, like a happy, lonely puppy excited to see his owner. "Miss Britain went to her cabin," Austin said, taking Maggie's coat from her.

"Ms," Jackson corrected.

"She was tired," Darlene volunteered.

"Not as tired as I am. I just barely flew in from New York yesterday, plus I had a three-hour layover. I drove straight here from Colorado. Talk about exhausting."

"Where were you flying from?" Austin asked.

"Paris, my dear. Oh, what a lovely city. And there are painters there too. You know, the ones that do portraits like they did in the old days. I had one done of me." Jackson walked over to the fireplace to build a fire. Maggie had a way of going on and on. His movement didn't slow her talk any. "The artist begged me, actually. I didn't have enough time, but he looked so hopeful that I'd do it, I hated to disappoint him."

"Yeah, he wanted to make enough money for dinner that night," Austin said. He was kicked back in his chair, his foot crossed over his opposite leg, arms folded.

Maggie darted him a glare then said, "Absolutely not. He paid *me* to pose for him. He'll be mailing me the painting. You should've seen how excited he was when I told him I'd do it. He looked like he won the jackpot on Jeopardy. You'll have to come see it when it arrives. I'm positive you'll love it. You always have a great eye for quality, and Phillip Frances is one of the best. I do miss having you around home. All the girls ask about you. You could have any three or four you'd pick. They'd be so thrilled to have your attention, they wouldn't even mind sharing."

"Mom!"

"It's true."

Darlene raised her eyebrows, but Austin answered his mother by shrugging. "Mom, I thought you wanted to move," he said.

Maggie laughed. "I tossed that around, but Michael thought we should . . ."

"Michael! Who's he?" Jackson dropped the fire poker, making a loud clanging sound. He picked it up, knowing his face was stormy with anger.

"Oops." Maggie brought her hand to her lips.

"Mom!" Austin stared at her. "What does 'oops' mean?"

"Calm down, Austin." Maggie patted the air as if signaling a dog to sit. "Michael is just a friend who stays with me when I'm in the states. But after I came home from France this time, I was frantic to see you." She reached across the table and grabbed Austin's chin.

He swatted away her hand. "Don't."

"Don't you understand?" Maggie asked. "I'm free now. I come and go with whoever I want and stay for as long as I want."

"I see." Jackson dropped the log on the hearth and wiped his hands. "That's what we were to you? Silly entanglements."

"Oh, sweetheart, don't get so dramatic. I love you. You know that. My reliable Jackson."

"Your security blanket."

"Well . . ."

———

"Excuse me," Darlene said as the discussion continued. No one appeared to hear her as she arose and hurried out of the room, slamming the door. Outside, the quiet wrapped around her with a tight grip. It was as if a man encircled his whole hand around her, choking, causing her to struggle to breathe. She ignored it and continued walking through the trees in Jackson's backyard.

Maggie, Jackson, her mom, her dad—all of them were doing everything wrong. Why were they making such messes of their lives? They should have figured it out by now. Her mom had been too weak; that had been her error. She had put on the airs of a strong, independent woman, especially when she talked about her work and standing up to the "men" in the university scene. But the truth was, the men were worn-out old guys who were too tired from years of battling students to have any fight left.

Her father had walked all over her mom, and Darlene had never once seen her mom stand up for herself. He'd fuss about dinner, and instead of saying, "If you don't like it, do it yourself," like Darlene would have said, her mom frantically searched the cupboard for something to satisfy him. It was like that when they talked about ideas, concepts, people, or which piece of furniture to put in the front parlor. Her dad had grown disgusted with a doormat for a wife and left to find someone more like "his Darlene."

Darlene knew she was feisty and took pride in her drive to make the world fairer for women. When she had stood up to her father, telling him he was "a deplorable male chauvinist pig" or "a domineering dictator," he had stared at her with shock. Then slowly, amusement spread through him, and he'd laugh at his failed effort and the fact that she called him on it.

Her mom would mumble, "I could never get away with that," but Darlene knew it was an excuse. Her mom never had the strength to stand up to him.

After watching Jackson with Maggie, Darlene decided he was as weak as her mother. Maggie was the extreme opposite—a flat-out bully. All these thoughts raced through her mind as she passed the mailboxes. She heard distant laughter of children, but it was the deep voice of Austin that caused her to look up.

His sharp brown eyes stared at her with the intensity of the stormy sky rolling toward them. "Hello," he muttered, his head hanging low and his brown, tousled hair blowing at the wind's whim.

The image of a beaten dog came to Darlene. "What are you doing?" she asked, trying not to signal she noticed his pain.

"Walking and thinking, the same as you."

"Then have you figured out that our parents go about living their lives all wrong?"

Austin chuckled. "Yeah, I figured that. I was just thinking how amazing it is they manage to make such a big mess of everything."

"Amen. They don't have to make everything so hard," Darlene said, walking with him in the opposite direction she had been going.

"My mom is a good person." Austin changed the subject abruptly as if he had to explain his family. "When I was little, she always taught me right from wrong. Once she took me to a prison and told me I never wanted to go there."

"I guess I lucked out," Darlene said. "My mom never did that."

Their shoes crunched against the rocks on the dirt road, a sprinkle of rain falling on them every now and then.

"Well, it made an impression on me." His voice was so soft, Darlene could barely hear the words, and she guessed that he was having trouble with his mom admitting that she was here one day and gone another. His dad might want his mother back, but even if he won her, it didn't look like she'd be staying long.

Austin's square jaw was drawn tight, and he stared fiercely, his face a black thundercloud. "My mom's lost."

———

Camille found the pounding on the door irritating. She wanted to scream, "Go away," but realized nothing would chase the person behind the knock away. When she pulled open the door, a soggy Jackson stood before her, eyes downcast and shoulders slumped.

"What?" she choked out, flushing red at the memory of his stunning wife.

"You won the bet. I'm here to be your serviceman."

Camille stared at him blankly.

"Our bet about the evil spirit coming? Remember? Well, the evil spirit came. I can't pretend it didn't, so I'm at your mercy. You win."

Camille opened her door wider.

She waited for Jackson to sit on the sofa in the living room before making herself comfortable in the plump chair farthest away from him. He sat on the edge of his seat as if he wanted to bolt, scanning the room until his eyes came to rest on the wood cabinet. He stood and proceeded to make a fire.

"So the bet will be honored with you making a fire?" she asked, trying to come up with something clever to say.

Jackson glanced at her, sadness flickering across his face. "No. This is a favor for a friend. Besides, I owe you one for flubbing our afternoon."

"It's hardly your fault. You didn't know she was coming."

He sighed. "No, but I hoped she would."

"Wh—"

"I wanted her to be jealous. I've been leading you on the past couple of days."

"That's not tr—"

"Don't deny it, Camille. We've had more than friendly exchanges."

"Uh—"

"You're such a beautiful, interesting woman, I couldn't resist. I enjoyed our time together. I didn't think about her at all. Or not much. I like being with you."

"But . . ."

"But nothing, except I should've gotten my feelings straight sooner. Well?" he asked, staring at her chin.

"Well, what?" She twisted her fingers together.

"How do you feel about me?"

A picture of the gorgeous Maggie and her tempting eyes came to Camille. Jackson had given Maggie a look he could never give her, no matter how much she longed for it. It was time she accepted the facts and stop fantasizing her life away. He would go back to Maggie sooner or later. Camille knew he still loved his wife.

"You're not my type," she whispered.

"What's your type?"

"Intellectual."

"I'm not smart enough, huh? Just a stupid hick? I thought you were disappointed when Maggie arrived." He towered over her. "Was I wrong? I thought . . ." He backed away to the hearth and kicked it. "I should give up on women. I'd be better off chasing bears. Good day, Ms. Britain. Sorry I interrupted your Sunday nap."

———

The downpour of rain didn't relinquish its intensity. Instead, the rain continued to beat the weak areas of soil until the ground began to cave. Puddles formed, filled up, and then spilled thick streams across the muddy road. As if oblivious to the effects of weather, Austin never halted his step, nor changed his course. He ploughed on, the rain puddles drenching his Levis as Darlene's expressions shot through his mind. She seemed to understand, or at least was compassionate to him. He felt no condescension from her, and that was a welcome relief. The fact she hadn't pried into his family business was another relief. He hadn't wanted to talk about it. Besides, no outsider would ever get the whole dynamics of his family situation. It wasn't what it seemed.

Once they'd said goodbye, he'd continued to walk alone, but it wasn't long before he was back at the cabin being greeted by his mother. She stood in the doorway, a compact mirror in hand. "Oh, there you are," she squealed. She went to kiss him, gave him a once-over, and stepped back. "I'm glad I got to say goodbye to you before I left."

"Where are you going?"

His mother handed him her keys. "Be a dear and drive my car over here for me."

Austin knew this mood well. His mom was caught up in her own world, with her own agenda. He never would understand where her thoughts were or why she acted like she did, but he did know it would be foolish of him to ask her any more questions. She'd never paid a moment's notice to them when she got like this. She continued to rattle on about the rain and needing to go and whatever else was on her mind. Maybe this was the way women were. If that was the case, he'd never understand them.

Austin drove the car to his mom, held the full umbrella perched above her, and guided her to the car. There he opened the door for her and kept the umbrella as a shield until she made it safely into the car. After taking the umbrella, she smiled and blew him a kiss.

The pouring rain drowned out any sounds of the motor. Austin stood in the rain, staring after the car long after it had turned the corner and slipped away. He stayed that way until the front door opened and his father leaned out and asked, "What ya doing, boy?" The question snapped Austin out of his thoughts. He walked into the house, realizing for the first time he was drenched and cold. As he shed his wet clothing, his father asked, "Did she go?"

Austin didn't answer. His fingers were numb, and he struggled to untie his boot laces.

"That's just like her," his father continued, "waltzing in, upsetting everything, and then waltzing out again."

Austin continued to work on his shoes, not wanting to get involved in this conversation. He'd hurry downstairs and get in the shower as his father fumed with emotions. But suddenly his father hooked him into the conversation by saying, "Give me your keys."

"Why?" Austin asked.

"Give them to me."

"But . . . you just wrecked your truck."

———

"What?" Darlene asked, trying to get her eyes to adjust to the dark in the kitchen, her hand on the phone. She was still half asleep. Maybe even dreaming.

"My dad. Have you seen him?" The voice sounded worried.

"My dad left me when he divorced my mom," Darlene mumbled and hung up the phone. A strong urge to cry came over her. "Dad," she whispered, making her way out of the kitchen.

She was almost to the staircase when the phone rang again. This time the dark ocean of sleep parted from her, and she realized it had been Austin on the phone. "Hello," she said into the receiver.

"Darlene, this is Austin. I'm not looking for your dad right now. I'm looking for mine. I want to know if he's over there."

"I was still asleep when I answered the first time."

"I could tell."

She rubbed at her eyes. "I don't think he's here. Why?"

"It's nothing."

Before she could say a word more, she heard the click of the phone.

"Who was that?"

Darlene flinched. She turned to see her mother standing on the stairway, clutching her bathrobe closed. "Austin. He was wondering if his dad was over here."

"At this time of night? Oh," she groaned. "This is all my fault."

"What are you talking about?"

"We had an argument tonight. Or last night. Whatever it was."

Darlene knew what she meant. She had no idea of the time, either. "He wouldn't desert Austin because you guys had a disagreement."

"He was upset."

"I was at their cabin, remember? It got even worse after you left. That lady declared freedom meant going wherever your instincts take you."

"She didn't."

"She did."

"Oh, poor Jackson."

"Poor Austin," Darlene said.

"Austin. How did he take it?"

"Hard. He told me earlier he thought his parents would get back together. It was a real shock for him."

"I can imagine," Camille said. "And now his dad has disappeared. We can't leave him alone. Let's go keep him company. He may not want us, but it's better than waiting and worrying by himself."

It didn't take long for them to drive to the Armstrongs' cabin. The darkness of the night pressed on them as the car's headlights cut through its dismal mood. The rain had changed into snow in the late hours of the night, and Camille drove with tension apparent in her face as she clenched and unclenched her jaw, driving cautiously and mumbling the whole way about the icy roads.

Darlene waited to ask her question until her mom had stopped the car and they were walking up to the Armstrongs' front door. "What did you and Jackson fight over?"

"Nothing. I was tired and so was he. Look, the house has so many lights on, it appears like it's on fire. Poor Austin must be worried sick."

Camille's guess wasn't far from the truth. Austin greeted them with his hair a tousled mess and the color drained from his face. Every time he sat down, he'd shoot back up and ask, "Where is he?"

"I don't understand. His truck was damaged. How could he fix it so fast?"

"He took my truck," Austin said. His face clouded over as he said this.

"You need to sleep," Camille said, taking him by the shoulders. "Your father is a grown man and he'll be okay. Walking around, running yourself ragged is not going to do you any good." Austin began to protest and Camille countered it by saying, "Your father is responsible. He'll come back."

"Then why hasn't he called? He has a cell."

"He might not have reception. Don't you worry." She patted him on the forearm. "But you really must get rest. We'll wake you if we hear any news. Promise."

"But I don't think I can—"

"Nonsense. Hop in bed. Do I have to come to your room and babysit until you go to sleep?"

"No, ma'am."

Darlene watched as Austin turned back to his room. At the click of his door, her mother began walking up and down the hallway, past the ugly brown, white, and black cowboy hats decorating the walls. Fighting sleep, Darlene watched her pace until six in the morning.

CHAPTER NINE

The anxious energy in the room shifted up several gears. Camille looked up from the breakfast she was preparing. Austin stood silently cast in the yellow rays of the early morning light, his hair tousled in sharp peaks as though each point represented a decimal or two of the headache pain he was probably experiencing. His face looked worn and heavy, as if he had aged to forty over the long night.

"Heard anything?" his voice rasped out.

"Sorry," Camille said, unable to maintain eye contact with him. She went back to chopping mushrooms for the omelet. "Breakfast will be ready soon." That was a stupid thing to say, but what else could be said? *Focus on the mundane—bring a sense of groundedness to this situation,* she advised herself silently.

"He didn't even take his wallet. I found it on top of his dresser. Why didn't I ask him where he was heading?" Austin asked, scratching his head. "That one simple question and we'd know where to search."

"You didn't know," she said. This was a tough thing for a boy to take on. "Can you make a list of places he liked to go? We can look for him after we eat."

"I wish I knew what they were," Austin said. "My dad only moved

122

out here a couple of months ago from the city. I came to visit him for the first-time last week."

"What city?" she asked.

"Denver."

She dished him up a plate of eggs and burned bacon. He wolfed the food down and headed toward the back door the same time Darlene, who had gone outside to peek at what the weather looked like, ascended the stairs. Both of them stopped short at the sight of Maggie approaching on the walkway, wearing tight jeans with a white, low-cut blouse. Her pulled-back curls showed off a perfect forehead and penetrating green eyes. "Can I talk with Jackson?" she asked breathlessly.

"No." Camille grabbed her coat and handed Darlene hers.

Maggie glanced at her son. "Where's your father?"

He flushed and then stammered, "Dad left for a drive last night and never came home."

"What do you mean never returned home? You make everything sound so dramatic. He probably left for Colorado to be with me."

"What are you doing here?" Darlene asked, stepping around Austin onto the porch. "Didn't you say you were leaving for home last night?"

"Well, yes," Maggie said. "I did. But the snowstorm stopped me. It really came down last night."

Wind twisted and blew through them, as if determined to let everyone know of its foul mood. Normally Camille would have suggested they talk inside, but she didn't want Maggie to stay longer than was necessary. "If that's the case," she said, "then we need to get searching for him immediately." She sidestepped everyone and hurried toward her car, Darlene trotting behind her.

"I told you he went to Colorado to see me," Maggie called through the wheezing wind. She stomped her snow boots back to her car. "His truck is powerful, and he was determined. There's no way he didn't make it out of here."

"Good. I am glad to hear it." Camille slammed her car door. She didn't feel like telling the woman he wasn't in his old truck, but in his son's, which might not be as reliable.

Darlene also shut her door but rolled down her window. "Austin, want to come with us?" she called.

"He's with me," Maggie said.

Darlene looked at Austin, and when he didn't speak, she rolled up the window. "I don't like that woman," she muttered.

Camille gripped the steering wheel as she drove through the snow. "If it makes you feel better, I don't either," she confessed.

The girls drove around aimlessly in the snow for a couple of hours, watching for Austin's truck. By noon there was still no sign of Jackson, so they decided to return to Camille's cabin. The phone rang as they climbed out of the car, and Camille scrambled to answer. "Hello. Hello. Anyone there?" She gasped into the phone.

"Camille, is that you?"

"Who's this?"

"Oriana—your long lost friend."

Yes, Oriana, the reason she was here at this cabin in the first place. "How are you? And your daughter? I've been thinking about you."

"Cindy had her baby and they both made it. Can you believe it? Her baby is in intensive care right now, but he's alive!"

"That's wonderful news."

"Thanks. How's your stay at the cabin? Are you getting the rest you've needed?"

"Oh, thank you so much for lending me your cabin rental." Camille propped her elbows up on the table. "Actually, I'm more tired than ever, but it is beautiful here. I'll tell you everything when I get back."

"I hope it involves a man."

"We'll see."

"Ooh, how exciting! I knew you were supposed to have the cabin. I can't explain, but I sensed it."

"We'll have to see if you're right," Camille said. There was a beep on the phone. "Oh, that's my other line. I better take it. Thanks for calling and sharing your wonderful news." Camille frantically searched for the phone's flash button. "Hello?" No one was there. What if it had been Jackson? Or the police calling to tell her he was dead? Beads of sweat bubbled on her forehead.

"Let's go to the Westguards and see if they know anything," Camille said to Darlene, who was shedding her coat.

"Why would they know anything?"

"I don't know. I can't just sit here."

The snow squeaked under the pressure of the tires. The puffy flakes still slept on most of the land except where cars had trespassed on the beauty. Neither Camille nor Darlene stated the obvious: Jackson was probably stuck somewhere in the woods, trapped in drifts, hurt.

At the Westguards', Camille pounded the door. Phyllis answered, "Oh, Camille and Darlene, come in. I want to hear all about your adventures in Yellowstone. Did you have a good time with Jackson?" She smiled knowingly at Camille.

"Yes, but we've come to talk about Jackson," Camille said.

"Ah, you want more information about the man with the big aloha? You two must be getting pretty serious. How wonderful!" She clapped her hands. "This would make Jackson's mother so happy. I was friends with her long ago before she died. I know when she peeks down from heaven and glimpses him, she must surely shudder. The poor woman didn't believe in divorce. My, how the world has changed."

"Jackson's missing," Camille blurted out.

Phyllis's eyes narrowed a crack, as if trying to see if Camille was joking. She looked at Darlene, who nodded confirmation. "Whatever do you mean?"

"He never came home from a drive last night."

"How odd."

"We've searched everywhere we could think of," Darlene said. "I'm getting so worried my stomach won't stop knotting."

"You poor child," Phyllis said, embracing Darlene. "Jackson knows how to survive in this country. Have you tried calling the Quick Response Service?"

"We haven't," Camille said. "I knew you'd know what to do."

Jackson awoke, screaming in the early morning sunlight. Extreme pain shot through his body in sharp, piercing jabs. He tried to move his right leg, but the ache intensified. A wave of dizziness fell over him. *Stay awake,* he told himself, willing his eyes open. When they did flutter wide, everything around him was blurred. Forcing himself to be patient, he focused on an object until he figured out it was a black gearshift.

Trickles of heat blew on him from the vents. *The vehicle must still be on,* he thought, overcome by a crashing wave of agony. His eyes closed and he swallowed a scream. Once he mustered control over the unrelenting stabs, he glanced at a yellow Christmas tree air freshener dangling from the rearview mirror. Austin's truck. Why was he there? What had happened?

———

"Find out anything?" Darlene asked before Camille had replaced the phone on the receiver.

"There have been dozens of accidents in the area," Camille said.

Phyllis gasped. "Dozens?"

"The paramedics were busy all night, and the cops are patrolling the area for stranded vehicles. The snow turned the roads into skating rinks. Lots of cars spun out of control, even when the drivers traveled slowly. And—" *And,* Camille thought, *Jackson was upset and angry at me, so he probably wasn't traveling slowly.*

"And what?" both Phyllis and Darlene asked.

"One died. A mother of two children."

Darlene rushed out of the room. The bathroom door slammed shut.

"Up for herbal tea?" Phyllis asked.

"I'll help."

Camille sipped her tea until the pounding in her chest became almost unbearable. "I need to go to my car and find Austin's phone number. I want to see if he's heard anything."

"I can give you the number," Phyllis said.

"Please, don't bother. I think a breath of air will help."

"I understand," Phyllis said.

This kind lady understood without her needing to make any confession. *That was nice,* Camille thought, slipping into the car. She sat on the passenger side where Jackson had been the day before, stroking the fabric. She longed to be with him and have him hold her in his strong, protective arms. She loved his joking manner, his recklessness and unpredictability. She could almost see him with a teasing glint in his eye, chin tipped slightly back, amusement racing through his face as she made another stupid comment about superstition. She leaned back and peered at the roof of her car, remembering the strong link between them and how he could see into her soul. Where could he be?

———

A rustle drew Jackson from unconsciousness. A distant boom echoed through the cold. Perhaps a door? Voices converged in a mumbled stream, drifting into Jackson's consciousness. He had an unexplainable feeling something was wrong. Every sense heightened: the dryness in his mouth, the chill prickling his skin, the ray of sunlight pouring on top of his closed eyelids. He strained to decipher the low hum of human voices.

"Looks like we have a bad one. Call for backup. The front of the truck's crushed in."

Crushed? Where was he? The coppery scent of blood hit his nose. Where'd it come from? His body throbbed with pain that seemed to come from everywhere. Becoming nauseated, he leaned forward and emptied his stomach. The bones around his knee shifted to contorted angles as a violent burst of agony palpitated through him. Tremors shook his whole body as he slumped into his seat.

Someone opened the car door. "Are you—?" The lady cursed. "We have to get him out of here fast. He's lost a lot of blood. Call for a helicopter."

"But where can it land?" A male voice.

"There's a clearing not far from here. We'll load him there."

Jackson groaned, feeling like an interloper listening to a faraway conversation.

"You're going to be okay," the lady said, patting his arm. "We'll get you to the hospital in no time."

"W—what happened?" he stammered.

"Are you allergic to anything?"

"No."

"Get authorization for Demerol," the lady yelled.

"Got it," someone called, farther away. Seconds later a needle poked in his hip, burning.

"Am I . . . okay?" He swallowed, forcing the rush of dizziness away as the sting in his hip faded.

"You'll be fine," the paramedic answered. "Now we have to get you out. You broke your femur, so it'll hurt."

He nodded, forcing himself to sit. He peered at his leg and glimpsed a jagged bone sticking through his jeans. His eyes closed and a cloud of blackness fell over him. Later he awoke to the feeling of a cold, slimy texture spreading around his knee.

"Welcome back. You're out of the truck, so the hardest part's over."

He nodded in a blurry haze. His responses seemed to have shifted to slow gear. He tried to wipe his face. His hand wandered around, not making a connection. The drugs must be taking effect, though the throbbing ache persisted. Voices talked above him in a dazed, erratic way.

"Ace bandage."

"Traction."

He was bound on a backboard with Velcro squeezing his sides. The EMTs grunted as they lifted him.

"Sorry," someone said.

He blinked in response. They lifted him onto the gurney and wheeled him inside the ambulance. The silver interior closed in on him. The paramedics talked on the phone as another wave of nausea overcame him.

———

Austin and Maggie stopped by the Britains' cabin early in the evening. Camille had to admit that Maggie, her hand twisting erratically, looked worried. The stress seemed to sink into her eyes, creating saggy bags underneath. "I can't believe he's not back. This is so unlike him." She slumped onto the couch. "He's been acting strange lately."

"Not quite so predictable anymore?" Camille said. The instant the words fled from her mouth she wished she'd thought first.

"What?"

"Nothing."

Maggie raised her eyebrows, her skin color deepening. "He's been talking to you, has he?"

"We're friends," Camille returned.

"I see. Well, Austin, we've done all we can for one day. Let's wait for your father at the cabin."

Austin shrugged and reached for the coat he'd tossed behind the cushion. Darlene touched his arm. "Your father's got to be okay. Everything's going to be all right."

"Oh, how sweet," Maggie said, twirling her keys around her finger as she whisked out of the room.

"Sorry," Austin whispered before he darted away. The door slammed after them.

"She didn't have to be so rude," Darlene choked out.

"I'm sorry, dear. I upset her . . ." The ringing phone interrupted her. Camille answered. "Hello?"

"Yes, this is the Quick Response Service, and we have a note here to call you if a white male approximately two hundred and fifteen pounds and about six-three was found."

"Yes."

"We've located a person who fits that description. We haven't been able to I.D. him. There was no identification in his truck, and he's not answering our questions."

"So he's alive?" Camille rested her hand on the rough countertop.

"Yes, ma'am, but as I was saying, we aren't positive it's the man you reported missing."

"What color was his truck?"

"Let's see . . . the report says blue, a jacked-up Ford."

"That fits. What happened to him? Will he be all right?"

"He collided with a tree and fractured his femur. Right now they're Life Flighting him to the Idaho Falls hospital. He'll undergo surgery on his leg but should be fine."

"How long will that take?"

"About two hours. Any more questions?"

"No. Thanks for calling. You don't know how relieved we are."

"You're welcome."

Camille hung up, aware of Darlene watching her. "What are we going to do?" her daughter asked.

"I don't know if we should go. We aren't really . . . what we should do is call Maggie and Austin. They need to know immediately. He will want his family there when he wakes." If it had been just Maggie, she wouldn't call, but Austin needed to know that his father was all right. She dialed their number and let the phone ring and ring. "No one is there," she said, hanging up. "We should leave a note at their place. I wonder where they are?"

"Maggie probably decided to get a manicure," Darlene retorted.

After they both laughed, her daughter looked at her seriously. "Mom, if we don't find them, Jackson will be alone in all that pain. That's not good."

"I'm sure we'll find them. We'll leave them a note."

"But what if they don't get it?" Darlene asked.

Camille's own worry made her unable to think clearly. She shoved her research books in her suitcase and said, "If we can't find Maggie and Austin in the next fifteen minutes, we'll go ourselves." That satisfied Darlene.

Camille had been sure that she would find Jackson's family, but her hunch was wrong and before she knew it, they had posted a note on Jackson's cabin door and were on the road.

An hour later, Camille and Darlene walked down a white hall, searching for the waiting room. A snowstorm had crept behind their car the entire way to Idaho Falls, and now, under the protective structure of the hospital, it had caught up with them. A tired nurse, sipping coffee from a Styrofoam cup, informed them Jackson was still in surgery.

"The orthopedic surgeon met the helicopter and they rushed him in immediately," she said. "But there's no need to worry. He's in very good hands. Dr. Roberts is one of the best. I'll have him come out and talk to you when he's finished. It'll be a while, though."

Camille and Darlene settled in the waiting room. Camille's attention wandered from the noisy television set, to the clerk's desk, to others that waited, and finally to the outside window where snow danced in the wind. Why had she been so unkind to Jackson? She leaned forward and rested an elbow on her leg. Warmth pressed on her shoulder as Darlene laid her hand there. Camille nodded to her daughter, giving her a weak smile.

When Dr. Roberts entered the room, he cleared his throat before asking, "Are you Mr. Armstrong's family?" He shoved his hands partially into the pockets of his blue scrubs.

Worried the doctor wouldn't let her visit Jackson, she said, "Yes . . . no, but I've been helping out with his son, and he'll want to see me." Her neck muscles tightened.

The doctor nodded, his gray hair slightly moving. "Where's the boy?"

"He'll probably be here tomorrow with his mother. They were gone when we received the news." The doctor appeared confused but didn't ask any more questions. "Is Jackson all right?" Camille searched the emotionless canvas of the doctor's face. His skin held a weathered texture with the flare of an experienced and knowledgeable professional.

"The surgery went well. He fractured his femur, so we inserted a metal rod into his right leg."

"A rod?" Camille asked.

"It's about as thick as your thumb. It goes from his hip to his knee."

"This rod is on the outside of his bone?" Camille questioned.

"No, through the marrow."

"Ouch," Darlene said. "He'll have problems getting through the metal detectors at the airports."

The doctor considered her daughter's comment with a furrowed brow. "That's true. That's really all I can tell you without his permission."

"May we visit him?" Camille asked.

"He'll be awake in an hour. Then it should be fine."

The doctor stepped backwards. "If that's all, I have other patients to attend to."

"Of course, thank you," she said. The doctor hurried away. Turning toward Darlene, Camille said, "Since we have an hour to wait, let's get Jackson a few magazines and food for when he's feeling better."

An hour later the women stood in the back of a long line. "Who'd have thought the grocery store would be packed?" Camille asked, tapping her hand on the handrail of the cart.

Darlene agreed, scanning the lines. "Probably a snow day at school or something."

"I hope he doesn't wake up before we get there."

"You can call and see if he's awake if you want," Darlene suggested.

Minutes later, Camille decided to leave Darlene in line to pay for the groceries. Dialing the hospital, she shivered in the Idaho wind outside of Albertsons. The receptionist said he was awake and asked if she'd like to talk to him. She swallowed the lump in her throat and said yes.

A strained voice answered.

"Hey trouper," she said. "You almost got yourself killed." She forced herself to be chipper.

"Who is this?"

She swallowed. "Camille. Are you okay?"

There was a slight hesitation before he answered. "I hurt, but I'll be fine." His voice sounded slow, drugged. And sleepy.

"How did it happen?"

"What?"

"The accident."

"Would you believe another moose jumped in front of me?"

She was glad to hear a bit of amusement in the words, even though his voice was still slow. "You're a moose magnet."

"Guess I am."

"You know what they say: the third time's a charm," Camille added.

"Great. I can't wait to get behind the wheel again. You're going to have me freaked out with that superstition stuff. Wait a second," he said. Camille heard him ask for a nurse. "How's Austin doing anyway?" he said, coming back to the conversation. "Do you know?"

"Yes. He was a tired mess when I last saw him. He's with his mother, searching for you. We were all pretty scared."

"Sorry."

"Your ex-wife broke into tears."

"She did?" He paused as though absorbing the information. "My ex-wife cried and you didn't?"

Camille swallowed hard. What was he asking? "Jackson, I'm sorry about yesterday."

"About what?"

"I wasn't being completely honest with you . . ."

"I'm listening."

Her heart pounded and the echoing pulse vibrated in her ears. She had promised herself she'd make it up to Jackson, and the spotlight was on. "I've felt more for you . . . than friendship . . . I'm lousy at expressing my feelings."

"You're risking them now."

"I know. But keeping my mouth shut causes everyone pain, including myself."

"That's quite . . . a conclusion there."

"It is. I've been doing a lot of thinking since yesterday. I was wrong." She wanted to add that no matter the pain, she wanted to take that risk with him, but she couldn't.

"I'm glad. I'd hate being the only one having feelings for a person."

Camille knew exactly what he meant. "Hey, Darlene and I got you some wildlife magazines, Cracker Jacks, a Slurpee, and stuff. Would you mind if we came by and dropped it off?"

He readily agreed, and Camille hung up to face her daughter's sour expression. *What is up with her?* Camille wondered.

They didn't speak until they were on the road, and the first thing out of Darlene's mouth was a complaint. "Ah, Mom, I overheard part of your conversation. Don't you think you're getting a little too cozy with Jackson? And for a person who thinks Grandma drives too fast, you're going warp," Darlene added.

Camille glanced at the speedometer. Her daughter was right. She was driving awfully fast, especially in the snow, but even still it was strange for Darlene to whine about it. "Hey, you're the one who wanted to come here to make sure he was okay."

Darlene pursed her lips and flipped on the radio.

"Is there something bothering you?" Camille asked. She could almost taste the thickness in the car.

Her daughter went silent for a long time before hesitantly saying, "I only wanted to come here because of Austin and because Jackson seems like a nice guy. But you need to know that he doesn't want to be divorced. He's trying to get back with that witch. He's been leading you on."

——————

Everything seemed to blur together, and actual events composed an only distant reality for Jackson. Muffled chatter of doctors and nurses and visitors echoed from the halls. Smells of sweat, blood, and antiseptic mixed with the throbbing pain from his leg. Finally a heavy blanket of sleep wrapped around him, taking him away from all those senses to thoughts and images of Camille, which were abruptly transposed with thoughts and pictures of Maggie.

Later, much later, the sensation of the automatic blood pressure machine squeezing his arm woke him. The IV in his arm pinched, and he resisted the urge to yank the needle out. He sipped water, listening, hearing, smelling. Then the blanket of sleep wrapped back around him.

CHAPTER TEN

Neither Camille nor Darlene spoke during the rest of the trip to the hospital. There, they found Jackson in a hospital bed, his head resting against a pillow, his injured leg propped on top of the sheets and blankets. Ace bandages covered the injury, along with a plastic gadget that hooked to his leg, collecting blood. IV cords flopped over the metal slats of the bed.

"Hello," Camille said, noticing he was pressing the button to squirt more medicine into his veins. The pain he was suffering must be horrible. Before Jackson could speak, a nurse came in and asked if everything was all right. She checked the IV and wrote on her clipboard.

"When's lunch?" Jackson asked the nurse.

"We'll check with the doctor and see if we can put more sugar in the IV. You're on a liquid diet today."

"Does that mean he can have this strawberry Slurpee?" Camille asked.

"If he feels up to it, but don't tell the doctor." The nurse winked.

Camille held up the Styrofoam cup and asked, "Would you even want it?"

"Are you kidding? I'd love it."

"That proves my hypothesis," Darlene said, grinning. "No matter what, men will never give up an offer of food."

"She's got that right," Jackson said, taking the cup Camille handed him.

Camille pointed to the flesh-toned bandage covering the IV needle in his arm. "What happened?" She'd never seen nurses use anything but the see-through tape.

Jackson flushed. "I can't stand seeing needles poking into me." He sipped the Slurpee.

"Are you all right? What's the pain like?" Camille asked.

"Deep," he whispered. "Real deep."

"I'm sorry."

"Thank you," he said.

"You know good luck is bound to come sometime," Camille said.

"Just like I was bound to come," said a voice from the door.

Camille turned to see Maggie and Austin. Maggie wore clingy fabric that accentuated her curves. In contrast, Austin seemed to be wearing the same shirt and jeans that he'd been wearing the last time she'd seen him. His face was haggard with lack of sleep.

"Dad, are you all right?" Austin hurried to his father's bedside.

"Yeah."

"You had me going for a while."

"Sorry. I'm also sorry about your . . ." Jackson's voice trailed off.

Color rapidly drained from Austin's face. "My truck?"

"Just a couple of scratches. I'll fix it better than new. Promise."

Austin didn't respond.

Camille moved out of Austin's way. She didn't notice that Maggie had come closer to Jackson until she bumped into her. A heavy scented perfume filled the air. "Oh," Camille said, excusing herself to the small couch.

Maggie cleared her throat and brushed at her outfit before saying, "Jackson, your son isn't the only one who's glad you're all right. I've worried myself sick."

Camille was feeling pretty sick herself.

Maggie brushed past Austin and threw herself across Jackson's chest. "My dear, I'm so happy you're all right," she muttered between the kisses she plastered on his cheek, leaving red lip prints.

Camille leaned over in an effort to catch Jackson's expression, but Maggie's blonde hair had tumbled to the side, blocking her view. Jackson did place his hand on Maggie's shoulder. Camille's back straightened. After clearing her throat, she said, "I must get going."

Maggie continued passionately kissing Jackson, slowly edging her way toward his lips.

"Darlene, shall we allow this family some privacy?" Camille struggled to say.

Her daughter nodded, and they both slid out of the room.

"Mom?" Darlene asked as they started down the hall.

Camille kept walking. She needed to be under the snowy afternoon sky.

"Mom?"

She increased her pace, and Darlene had to jog to keep up. "Mom, slow down."

"We need to hurry," she said, a bit breathless. If Darlene was right, and Jackson wanted his ex-wife back, it looked like he might have his wish. Maybe she'd imagined everything between them. Or maybe he had been leading her on.

She couldn't quite believe that. Jackson wasn't a man for that kind of behavior.

"Hey guys, wait up. Do you mind if I come with you?" Austin called from behind them.

"Sure," Darlene said.

"Will that be okay with you, Miss Britain?"

Ms. not Miss, Camille thought. Why couldn't the boy get it straight? "Of course you can come with us."

A throat cleared behind them, stopping Camille dead in her tracks. "Ms. Britain, could I have a word with you?" The feminine lilt of Maggie's voice was unmistakable.

Darlene instantly answered Maggie's question, "My mom's busy right now. We have to—"

Camille put her hand on her daughter's shoulder. "It's all right. I can spare a second to hear what she has to say." She handed her keys to Darlene. "Warm up the car for me, will you?"

Darlene hesitated, giving her mom a stare that plainly asked, *what are you doing?* Camille nodded for her to go on. Reluctantly, Darlene left, with Austin alongside her.

Camille turned her eyes on Maggie and stared, waiting.

Maggie fiddled with her hair before saying, "You know, Camille—you don't mind if I call you Camille, do you?" Without waiting for a response, she continued, "Jackson tells me that you were recently divorced. I don't know what happened, but if it was because of another woman, you'd know how I'm feeling right now."

"But you and Jackson are already divorced." Camille felt slow and stupid.

"Well, yes, but we both still have feelings for each other. Our relationship is fragile, and now with you on the scene our hopes of getting back together are shattering. Even Jackson feels this way. He told me that when you are around he gets all confused and doesn't know what he thinks about me."

Maggie wiped at her eyes with a tissue. "But you should know that even if things don't work out, Jackson told me he would never remarry. Sorry to have to tell you that. Jackson's never been one to do unpleasant chores."

With that, Maggie turned on her sexy high heels and walked back into Jackson's room. Camille stood in the hall. Despite her feelings toward Maggie, she did have a point. Though the two of them were divorced, Jackson did seem to still have a thing for Maggie, and that meant Camille had been acting like the other woman. Who'd ever thought she'd do that? Was that what being lonely had driven her to?

She would stay away from Jackson. If Jackson really wanted to get back with the annoying Maggie, she wasn't about to stand in the way of his dream.

The Giorgio scent filtered into Jackson's nose, drugging his senses. The aroma had always made him feel liquid with emotion and attraction. It sure beat skunk. The warmth of Maggie's lips pressed against his cheek. Maggie had returned to him with more feeling than he'd ever dreamed.

Then Camille spoke from the couch where she was sitting. In his drugged state, he didn't hear what she said, but it couldn't have had a more startling effect than if she'd poured a tub of ice water on his head. Betrayal and hurt oozed beneath her words. He knew that tone. He'd used the same tone when Maggie stood at their front door, bags packed.

Maggie started to nestle into his neck. This caught his attention. His grasp tightened on Maggie's shoulders as he pushed her away. "Maggie, please," he whispered as he scanned the empty room. "Where did everyone go?"

"What does it matter?" Maggie asked, stroking his cheek. "I've missed you. I'm glad they had enough sense to disappear, allowing us time alone." She bent to kiss him.

He held out his hand. "Stop."

"What?"

"I want to know where everyone is."

Her green eyes searched the room. "Camille and her daughter left. They said they had other plans." She hesitated before adding, "Oh, I forgot something in the car. I'll be right back."

While Jackson waited, he thought back to the morning when Camille had walked past his extended hand for the keys and said she could drive herself. So different from Maggie, who always insisted on being chauffeured. He had to admit he liked to be the driver. It felt natural.

He drifted until Maggie returned. With a loving smile, she sat on the corner of his bed, straightening her short skirt and crossing her legs. Jackson sensed her actions were calculating. He wished he wasn't so drugged up so he could understand what she wanted. "Maggie, why are you here?"

"I missed you, of course." She squeezed his good leg.

"You want more money. That's what it always is. I bet you only drove clear to Idaho so you could go shopping."

She stared at him before tucking her hands neatly on her lap. In a soft, stressed whisper, she said, "Did not."

"You left me." His lips pressed together. His leg throbbed, the jabs making him weary. "And now you have the guts to ask for money."

"Leaving was a mistake. A horrible one. I want you back, honey." She touched his forearm.

He pulled his arm away.

"Well?" she said.

"That's a hard one," Jackson choked out. His emotions seemed to be crashing down a waterfall. He had planned on fighting for her, on gluing back their marriage and their family.

"What's so tough?" She scooted closer. "You love me. We should be together."

"But do *you* love *me*?"

"I already told you I do, silly." She playfully hit him in the arm.

"Really?"

"Why do you question me?"

"Why did you leave?" Jackson shot back.

"I got restless."

"And what's going to stop you from getting restless again?" He wanted to ask about the man she'd obviously been carrying on with. How could he be sure that was over?

"I still want my freedom." Maggie sighed. "I figured we could work out an arrangement."

"Did you?"

"I know you want us to get back together. Austin assures me that you do. Is he wrong?" She patted his arm. "I want to be with you too. Believe me. And since you've shown a willingness to let me explore my creativity, why shouldn't we remarry? We could be happy. And it'll make our son happy. What do you think?"

"There's . . . nothing to say," Jackson said.

"Not a yes or a no or a let's-think-about-it?" She batted her long eyelashes.

140

"No ... nothing."

"I need to know, Jackson."

"Look, I've had a very long couple of days. I'm tired, I hurt, I'm drugged up—I can't even think straight right now, much less make any decisions." His thoughts went to Camille, and he couldn't help but wish it was her he was talking to instead of Maggie. She seemed to understand the pain.

"You need time. I respect that. Let's get you some clothes and bust this joint."

"He's not going anywhere for several days," said the nurse who stood at the door. "And I'm going to have to ask you to leave now. He needs rest."

"Very well." Maggie leaned over and kissed Jackson on the cheek and whispered softly, "I love you." With that she stood, bestowed on him her dynamite smile, and left.

———

The next morning Darlene sat by Camille on one of the queen beds in their hotel room.

"Yes?" Camille yawned. She'd somehow managed to calm herself last night enough to concentrate on her coursework, working so late that she fell asleep without having to think about Jackson and Maggie. She still didn't know what she was going to do. She longed to get away from Idaho and Island Park, but she didn't want to return home.

"Are you all right?" Darlene asked.

Sitting up, she said, "Why wouldn't I be?"

"*I'm* waking *you* up. What's wrong with this picture?"

Camille laughed. "I stayed up late working." She pointed to her books on the floor.

"Um," Darlene said. "I'm sorry about Jackson."

"What's there to be sorry about?"

"I know you were beginning to like him."

"It never would've worked. He's too controlling. An unpredictable cowboy. Do you remember how he freaked when I wanted to drive?"

Darlene smiled. "The Fourth of July explosion. His son's the same way."

"They'll take generations to evolve. If it's at all possible."

"Sad," Darlene said, making a long face.

"Hey, don't get depressed."

"I'm not. Just thinking."

"What about?" Camille asked.

"Is it possible for men and women to co-exist and not cause each other pain?"

"You think men experience pain?" she asked her daughter, remembering the cynical smile Adam had given her before slamming the door in her face. His heart seemed incased in iron.

"Dad does," Darlene whispered.

"What?"

"You heard me."

"Why did you say it?"

"He's a nervous wreck. All I hear is how hard it is to live alone. I told him I'm single and don't find it difficult. He said, 'It's different after you've been married.'"

"He's getting married," Camille said softly.

"This was before. You know, I haven't seen him since he started dating that woman. He's suddenly too busy for me."

"If he was so miserable being alone, why did he leave?"

"Mom!"

"I'm serious. We could've worked out our problems. I would've tried anything." Tears welled in her eyes, blurring Darlene's face. "Am I that bad that he'd rather be miserable than stay with me?"

"It's not like that."

"Yeah, right. Look, Darlene, I know you're trying to be nice, but please don't say any more."

"Mom, you're a wonderful person. Dad just—"

"Please, no more. I have a headache. Would you mind getting me an aspirin? Make it three."

"That's too many."

"This headache really hurts."

"I'll get you two pills. No more."

"Darlene!"

"I'm getting them." She dug in her suitcase, snatched a glass off the television, filled it with water, and handed her mom two aspirins.

After swallowing the pills, Camille chuckled. "You're a stubborn one too."

"It's in the genes." Darlene knelt by her suitcase to pack away her stuff. "Do you think Austin's okay? You didn't even wait to see if anyone was at his friend's house when we dropped him off there yesterday."

"I didn't?" Camille was stunned. "Oh, well, he's an adult after all and has his head on straight—mostly."

"You're saying that because he's going to college."

"And he's ambitious."

"Okay, okay," Darlene said, "enough about how wonderful he is."

Camille slipped into jeans and a cotton shirt. "Let's grab breakfast."

After eating, they drove around, soaking up the feel of the town. It seemed like any other city, with chain grocery stores, gas stations, and a mall. The snow had melted, leaving everything a muggy gray, which matched the feeling in Camille's heart. When they finally made it back to the hotel, Darlene decided to go jogging, and Camille went back to work.

―――――

Sleep was nonexistent for Jackson until he begged the night nurse for sleeping pills. Between the excruciating pain and his women dilemma, he'd gotten little rest. The Giorgio perfume lingered in the room, luring his thoughts to Maggie. Her lips were delicately curved, and she always wore thick pink or red lipstick. Her last three words remained imprinted in his memory. *I love you.* Once he had dreamed of hearing exactly that, but the elation he'd expected was nonexistent. He remained empty, like a football pass that had fallen short. Images of Camille's natural beauty crowded his mind. He pictured her sporty haircut and knowing eyes. She'd driven down from Island Park to see how he was. Of course, so had Maggie. *Well, for that or shopping,* he thought with a grimace.

One problem was the mixed messages Camille sent. She had coldly, without even a flinch of remorse or doubt, said she was not interested in him. Now when competition arrived on the scene, here she was. Was she being petty, only wanting something because another person wanted it? Of course, she hadn't put up much of a fight when Maggie had thrown herself at him. She'd simply left. Another important fact when it came to Camille was her fascination with superstition. That odd trait was neither normal nor healthy. Perhaps her husband had divorced her for good reasons. These thoughts twisted around inside him until he concluded he should give the whole thing up. He was much better off roaming the mountain. Life was a lot simpler without women and their guessing games.

Finally, the drugs did their job and sleep overcame him. He didn't feel rested when a nurse woke him some time later to take his vitals. "Dr. Roberts likes to do rounds at six in the morning when it's his day off," the middle-aged woman explained to the intern at her side. "He almost always shows up right on the button and is ornery if everything's not already finished."

"One of those king types, huh?"

"Not as bad as others," the nurse answered. "After you record the patient's vital information, check his water bottle. Don't want him dehydrating." They continued to talk as they walked down the hall, their voices growing more muted with each step.

Coldness enveloped Jackson. What were they trying to do, freeze him? He reached for the blankets that had fallen off during the night. Not being able to bend his right leg posed a problem. He struggled to grasp the fugitive blanket but couldn't. He lifted his good leg straight in the air, bringing with it a corner of the blanket. From there he pulled the blanket to his shoulders. The sheet remained entangled somewhere at the bottom of the bed. For the next fifteen minutes he lay in the bed, irritated he couldn't do one simple thing—fix the sheet —and that he had to use a bedpan. A door opened, flooding the darkness in the room.

"How we doing?" Dr. Roberts asked as he read the chart. He wore jeans and a red Polo shirt.

"What'cha gonna do for your day off?" Jackson asked, remembering that the doctor had mentioned that tomorrow was his day off.

"Ride horses up Taylor Mountain."

"Isn't it a little cold?"

"Not for the true horse lover."

"Sounds like my kind of outing," Jackson said. "I can't wait to go skiing this year. The weather people predict lots of snow. By the way, when am I going to be up and at 'em?"

The doctor put down the chart. He lifted Jackson's ankle and asked him to rotate it. "You won't be doing any sports for about a year and a half to two years. Can you move your toes?"

Jackson wiggled them. "What?"

"Your leg has taken a major blow, but it looks like you have most of the mobility back."

"Not all?"

"'Fraid not." The doctor flipped through papers on the chart. "Your temperature, blood pressure, and neuro-circulatory status are good, but you're losing a little more blood than normal. That's nothing to worry about. I'll have the nurses change the dressing. Are you ready for food?"

"Yes."

"I'll make a note and you'll be on the sign-up sheet for a delicious breakfast."

"That bad, huh?" Jackson asked.

"Let's just say most of the patients rely on family or friends."

"Great," Jackson mumbled, wondering who would help him. "What time's breakfast?"

"Between eight and nine. About ten o'clock, physical therapy will drop by and we'll get you on crutches and teach you transfers. It'll be painful at first. Your muscles don't want to work. But I'm sure you'll do fine. Are you having any other problems?"

"Can I get rid of this IV?"

"Sorry, you get to keep it for the next couple of days until your vital signs stabilize, then we'll put on a heparin lock. That's a little tube, and you won't have to deal with all the lines."

"Are you sure about sports?" Jackson asked.

"Absolutely."

"Would that include hiking?"

"You can only do lower-level hiking on flat or shallow trails. It's kinda rough, I know. I busted my leg playing basketball probably fifteen years ago."

"How'd it happen?"

"I twisted it going for a layup, and this big two-hundred-and-fifty-pound guy landed on top of my knee." The doctor moved toward the doorway. "Is that all I can do for you?"

Jackson nodded, hoping for sleep before breakfast. Breakfast arrived at eight twenty: a tray holding cold cereal, milk, orange juice, a blueberry muffin, and one slice of bacon. He ate it all, wondering if he'd starve. His normal breakfast consisted of three times more food, and he vowed that the first friend or family member to walk through his door would go on a food run. Of course, if it was Maggie, she would probably send Austin for the food. She'd never go herself.

Why did he find Maggie so attractive? She was beautiful, yes, but she was also unfaithful and selfish. Not to mention that she constantly picked at him. Camille had that superstition problem, but she seemed to like him as he was. Wasn't that love? Accepting someone with all their faults? He finished mopping up the crumbs on his tray. It seemed obvious that he'd been a fool with Maggie.

The thought had barely finished when Austin waltzed in.

"Hi," Jackson said.

"How you feeling?"

"I'm pretty drugged up, so I'm not doing too bad. Hungry, though."

"That's why I brought you two McDonald's Big Breakfasts. An order of pancakes and a mess of sausage with egg and biscuit."

"That's my man! How did you know?"

"Remember when I got my appendix out?" Austin paused. "What did the doctor say?"

"They're going to get me on crutches later today."

"Good news. I stayed over at the Smiths' house last night."

"What's happening with them?"

"Mrs. Smith dyed her hair purple and it looks funny. Besides that, nothing really."

"Where's your mom?"

"Don't know. Last I saw her, she and you were mushing each other." Austin smiled.

"I guess that's true." Jackson knew he should say something about that, but he didn't want to wipe the smile from his son's face. "Is Rusty being taken care of?"

"I dropped her off at the Westguards before headin' here." Austin picked at the napkin on top of Jackson's plate. "Have you seen Miss Britain?"

"No."

"It wouldn't surprise me if she goes home," Austin said.

"To the cabin?"

"No. Home, home. I hope she does. That lady is gonna get killed if she stays in the wild. Darlene told me how she tried to start a fire with lighter fluid."

A sound at the door made Austin and Jackson turn their heads. Maggie stood in the doorway wearing a light blue silk jumpsuit with thick shoulder pads and a cinched waist. The blue contrasted nicely with her china doll features and almost-platinum hair, which fell in delicate curls halfway down her shoulder. "I can do the wild," she said, smiling widely.

"Wow, you look great, Mom." Austin walked over to his mom and kissed her cheek. "You're really ready for the wild?"

"I'm always up for adventure."

"I'm not," Jackson said.

"That's okay." Maggie winked. "Because you're an adventure in yourself."

"That's not what you said in the past," Jackson said.

"I was wrong," Maggie replied.

Was he imagining it, or did her eyes not quite meet his?

———

After a painful morning trying to use crutches, Jackson collapsed into a heap on his bed, welcoming the rest. "I'm tired."

"I'm sorry you're hurting." Maggie patted him on the hand.

He gave a weak nod.

"Want us to get you lunch?"

"Yeah," Jackson said.

Maggie drifted over to the chest of drawers. "Jaxy, where's your wallet? Didn't Austin bring it to you yesterday?" She fumbled through his stuff beside the table until she realized it wasn't there. She slipped a twenty from her purse and waved it at her son. "Austin, why don't you get us something?"

He took the bill and headed out the door.

"Now," Maggie said, smiling as brightly as the sun. She edged over to Jackson and kissed him. Warm, velvety lips touched his. Sensations shot through him before he pulled away, his stomach swimming.

"What is it?" she asked.

"We need to talk."

"We can do that later. Austin will be back in a little while."

"That's why we need to talk now. You can't march out of my life after twenty-some-odd years and then return and think everything's going to be the same. It doesn't work like that." He propped his pillow and lowered his head onto it gradually.

"But you still love me." She caressed his cheek, her smooth fingers following his jaw line.

"I don't trust you."

"Why not? I'm here. I'm showing love. You can't doubt my feelings."

"Why can't I? You've been tramping all over the world with other men." She closed her lips and then opened her mouth to speak, but Jackson put his index finger to her lips. "Before you say any more, I want you to listen. If you want to be with me, I need commitment, and not just until you grow bored or depressed."

"But you're always so . . ."

His stomach clenched. There it was. She didn't really want him. It was the money. She was only telling him what he wanted to hear. "If you don't like the way I am, that's your problem. I don't know what I ever saw in you. Please leave."

"What do you mean? I traveled all this way to see you."

"Go," he snapped.

"I can tell you're not thinking straight. You need sleep. I'll be back later."

Maggie left, with no lingering looks or protests. Jackson was glad. He closed his eyes, hoping sleep would relieve the throbbing in his leg. But the pounding of his heart kept him awake.

Later, Austin sauntered in with KFC bags. "Where's Mom?"

"She left."

"Why?"

"She needed to think." He nodded at the bags in Austin's hand. "Are you going to let the chicken get cold?"

After eating, Jackson fell into an exhausted slumber, waking again when the door opened. A plump, smiling nurse waddled in. "We have flowers for you, Mr. Armstrong. Where do you want me to put them?"

"By the phone is fine."

The nurse did so, then handed him the card.

Fighting his eyes open, Jackson read the card. "Glad things turned out for you. Darlene and Camille."

———

Sitting down on the hotel bed, Camille dialed Oriana's number and was soon chatting with her good friend. After exchanging pleasantries, Camille learned how well Oriana's grandson was doing, and then Oriana changed the subject. "Well, out with it. Sounds like you're in a dilemma."

"What makes you say that?" Camille said, her heart rate increasing.

"Your voice. Nothing else would cause that forced friendly tone."

"You're right," Camille admitted, seeing no point in denying it. "There's this guy." She proceeded to go over the horrible Halloween, the unfortunate run-in with the skunk, and how Mr. Fix-It Man swooped to the rescue so he could use her car to go to Yellowstone. Then she told about Yellowstone, leaving out their mutual confessions. Lastly, she described Maggie. Maggie, the beautiful. Maggie, the gracious.

Oriana interrupted. "She might be a china doll, but you have brains."

"Which do you think men prefer?" Camille snapped.

"Not all men like the superficial outside with milk toast inside. Besides, you're a beautiful, healthy, smart lady. Not a slut or a user like his ex-wife seems to be."

"Thanks," Camille whispered.

"So what's up with this Jackson cowboy now?"

She described the accident. "I feel awful for him. He's had a lot of pain."

"It'll be all right."

"You don't understand. We had a fight right before. He told me he was interested in me, and like the fool I am, I told him I didn't care for him."

"You what? Why?"

Camille was helpless to explain. She had asked herself those exact same questions. Why did she do the things she did? None of it made any sense. "I don't know," she admitted. "I tried to fix it, but then Maggie arrived and they started kissing in front of me—"

"Kissing? What do you mean kissing?" Oriana asked. "On the lips?"

"Of course."

"Oh that's not good. What did you do?"

"I left."

"You mean, you quit."

"What could I do?"

"Kick up a lot of dust."

"Yeah, right. I'm sure that would look really good. A recently divorced middle-age woman trying to seduce a cowboy from an absolutely gorgeous woman, who happens to be his wife. Thanks, but no thanks."

"Okay," Oriana said, "but I think you're selling yourself short. If he's predictable, he'd like the stability you offer."

"That's just it. I *don't* think he's predictable. Reliable, yes. But reliable means he'd want to fight to keep his family together, doesn't it? Ugh." She heaved a sigh. "The smart thing for me to do is focus on my work and forget men—all men."

"That's a nice way to live. Bury your head and deny everything if life gets uncomfortable."

The statement struck Camille like a heavy blow. She knew she'd be thinking about it for quite a while.

After the phone call, she decided a hot bath with a touch of lavender would do wonders. Could Oriana possibly be right about Jackson needing her stability? Thoughts of Jackson standing tall against the closing day stuck in her mind. Against the sunset, that was how she'd first seen him. Finishing her bath and dressing, she slumped to the kitchen table and flipped open a book. She had to stop thinking about Jackson and work.

Once she made herself focus on her studies, her mind drifted from her problems. Work absorbed her. Today she studied Lewis and Clark as they neared Yellowstone. Lewis had climbed up a tremendous bowl, close to the border, and saw Yellowstone's valley and rivers and decided not to venture in that direction. If he had done so, he would've reached Three Forks weeks, maybe even months, sooner. Camille shook her head. A shame. What great picturesque views the explorers had missed because they decided not to risk and push a little farther to see where the path led.

John Colter wasn't willing to give up that direction, so he bolted upstream to the wilderness and mountains, while the others descended below. He etched his place in the history books as the first white man to discover Yellowstone. Many people did not believe his story of the beauty and the landscape, calling Yellowstone "Colter's Hell."

Camille tapped her pen on the notepad. Colter traveled the distance, and because others weren't willing to do the same, they doubted and poked fun. So like human nature. Was she doing the same thing in her relationship with Jackson? Oriana was right. She'd never know Jackson's feelings if she didn't ask him. He'd told her he had feelings for her. Was that the action of a man who was sure about pursuing his ex-wife? While his reaction to Maggie's kiss had appeared to be positive, he was taking a high dose of pain medication, and maybe his reaction was skewed. Besides, he might have been so surprised by Maggie's kiss he didn't know what to do. She would have been if Adam did that to her. She grabbed the phone to call him before the confidence had a chance to stew and start bubbles of doubt.

It rang once before she replaced the receiver. No, better to go over and see him herself. Then she would know for sure if there was anything between them.

CHAPTER ELEVEN

Maggie strung her perfectly manicured nails through the fuzz on the young boy's head. "There, there, Michael. The drugs will take effect soon." The little boy stared up at her from the hospital bed with clouded eyes and barely blinked his acknowledgement. She leaned forward on the mattress and gently kissed his clammy forehead. "I need to be going now, but I'll come back and visit you soon."

"Thank you," he whispered. His face held a strong flush of red.

Maggie smiled, pleased.

Now she had one more patient left to go. It took her several minutes to make her way across the hospital, then another several minutes of delay when she stopped in the restroom to freshen up. Satisfied, she went into room 174. The door was slightly open, so she eased her slender body through and cast her eyes on the big man lying on top of the snow-white crisp hospital sheets. Seeing someone who always represented the epitome of strength and manhood laid up in bed like a helpless, sick bird struck her. What an unusual sight.

"Oh, Jackson, darling, I've returned. Sorry I was gone so long. I've been visiting the cancer patients. Some of them just need encouragement."

He looked in her eyes, his expression unreadable. She pressed her skirt close to her and sat down in a chair near his bed. "Now, how is my favorite patient doing?" His bushy eyebrows raised, brown eyes peering out from under them. A common-looking man, but she had missed his consistency. *Funny,* she thought, *that was the same reason I left him.* Predictability did get boring. "Jackson, I'm sorry I caused you so much pain." His face whitened. "Really, I am. Let me make it up to you."

She waited, watching him close. He remained emotionless, except for a trace of red sprouting up his throat and face. "Say something."

"What do you want me to say?" he asked.

"That you don't hate me."

"I don't."

"But?"

"But, what?"

"Forgive me." She reached out and ran her fingertips over his frame. She continued, "I never wanted to hurt you."

He moved away from her. "Why did you?"

"I was going crazy."

"So I drive you crazy? Yet, you want me back. Or do you just want more money to spend with your lover?"

"I just made him up. I have no one in my life."

"Why would you do that?"

Her heart thumped as heat spread through her. How was she going to explain? "I, um, made him up because I was angry that you were with the professor lady. I thought after I left, you would . . ." *Come running after me. Begging. Pleading. Then I'd know you really loved me. That it wasn't just a game to you. If you loved me, really loved me, you would have known that.*

"Good grief." His angry voice broke into her thoughts. *"You were the person who left me. I had to get on with my life."*

She felt her chin tremble as she struggled to focus. She had been wrong. Jackson was too hurt to run after her. She would have to do patch-up work to make him feel loved again.

Maggie reached out and softly flipped his bangs off his forehead. "Jaxy, baby, I want to come back."

"What do you mean?"

"You know, be a couple again. Please." Maggie continued to play in his hair. She bent down and kissed him long, hard, and with emotion. That had always worked in the past. She thought she heard something through the open door, but when she looked over, no one was there. "Well, Jaxy?"

He sucked in his breath, but before he could say anything there was a muffled exclamation, apparently coming from the hallway. Maggie frowned, annoyed at the disruption. She was considering shutting the door when a large nurse shuffled into the room and said, "I'm sorry to break up the party, but Jackson needs to walk on his crutches."

Maggie kissed him again firmly. It worried her that he didn't quite respond, but he wouldn't hold out against her long. She knew him, his loyalty and his dependability. He had to give her another chance.

"I'll get you a snack," she said, "and come right back."

———

Camille apologized to the nurse outside Jackson's room, but she didn't halt her pace. The image of Maggie with her hand in Jackson's hair burned into her mind. She'd had it with stupid love games. Oriana was wrong, wrong, wrong about Jackson. It was time to get back to Island Park and focus on her teaching. Hopefully, she'd be finished before Jackson was able to leave his cabin—if he even went back there. She couldn't see Maggie living that kind of life.

Back at the hotel, she had almost finished packing when Darlene came back from the hotel's gym. "What's going on?" she asked.

"We're leaving. Please do check the room for everything while I close this suitcase."

"Mom, what's going on?"

"We're leaving."

"Mom, stop it. I can tell you're upset. What happened?" Darlene sat on the far bed. "It's Jackson, isn't it?"

Camille knew she must have gone completely pale. Darlene would need to drive.

———

The acute pain of working on rehabilitation stole all of Jackson's attention. The physical therapist taught him how to transfer from bed to crutches. After that they went over different exercises to strengthen and stretch his injured muscles. By the time he returned to his room, he was exhausted and sank wearily onto his bed. As he lay on the narrow mattress, recapturing his breath, he couldn't help thinking about Maggie's proposal. She had spoken with straightforward frankness, her eyes flashing and her chin lifting slightly in challenge. This left him feeling cold and shivering, although her proposal was what he had wanted. He didn't understand himself. Why was he feeling this way?

Maybe it was that ruthless, unyielding aura Maggie exuded. So unlike Camille. He'd bet his cabin she didn't have it in her nature to ever give that kind of impression. Even when she stubbornly refused to get in the truck on that rainy Halloween afternoon, her face pinched together in her anger, it had a different feel to it than the chilled-to-the-bone expression of his ex-wife's.

The phone rang, and he leaned over to grab it. "Hello?"

"Do you love my mom?" came a young girl's angry voice.

"What! Darlene?"

"Yes. Do you love her?"

"I—I—I—"

"Exactly what I thought. You're stomping all over her like she's some doormat, and I want it stopped. You're nothing but a male chauvinist pig who—"

"Hold on there, little lady, I'm not that kind of guy. I really like your mom. She's beautiful, intelligent, practical, self-confident—"

"Then why is she in tears? Why are you with that . . . Maggie? If you ask me, you're nothing but a sucker. Your wife's out sleeping with other men and she's stringing you along. You follow her like a sheep to the slaughter because she's pretty. Do you even like anything about her?" She didn't wait for him to answer, just plunged on. "I figure you're acting like this for one of two reasons. First, your pride. You're having a hard time being dumped. It flatters your ego, seeing her beg you to come back. The second is you're an enabler. If some cute girl jerked Austin around, sleeping with other boys, would you want him to stay with her? If you stay with Maggie, you're teaching him that's okay. Maggie isn't going to change while you are enabling her. Think about it, and stay away from my mom if you don't love her."

The line went dead as she hung up the phone.

———

The next morning arrived, and Jackson was more than ready. He hadn't stayed in a bed this long—ever. Besides, he hated being at the mercy of other people.

Maggie appeared right after he finished eating a muffin and cold cereal. "Ready?" she asked.

Not long afterward, they exchanged the stark white walls of the hospital for the dull grays of the morning. Jackson swung his body forward with exaggeration as he maneuvered his crutches to the car. Maggie laughed. Once they slipped into the vehicle, she wrapped her arm around him and rested her head on his forearm. "This place is such a rat hole. I'll be glad to get out. The closest real city around here is Salt Lake. That's only four hours away. Shall we?"

"I'm living in Island Park."

"I know, but I thought since we are together we could . . . you know."

"What?"

"Do something wildly romantic. An expensive steak dinner by candlelight with a fresh Caesar salad and a creamy double-decker dessert. Later we could check into one of those anniversary hotels or somewhere nice."

"Maggie, I have to live on a tighter budget."

"You could splurge this once. This is a special occasion." She batted her eyelashes.

He slumped forward. How had he forgotten about her bulldozing behavior, especially when it came to money? "Maggie, what are you talking about? I just got out of the hospital."

"Come on, I've stayed in this place long enough. It's hickville. There're no suitable hotels around here."

"Maggie!"

"What? If you're suggesting we stay here, I can't do it."

The heavy pressure of his wife's worry about looking perfect, always satisfying the invisible critics, double-checking her appearance and then complaining the diet pills didn't work—it all came crashing down on him. He understood now. Everything was always image with her. And with Camille, it was superstition. He was glad he didn't live his life confined by rules of superstition or image. He scrutinized his ex-wife. She wore tight white jeans and a flattering pink blouse. Then his gaze rose upward to where a frown etched into her face. What was he doing with this woman who had betrayed him? She controlled him like a yo-yo. What was he teaching his son? Darlene was right!

"Maggie," he said, "I've got a question that I'd like you to answer."

"What?"

"You said you were in Paris. Is that where all the money went? And if that is true, why did you call me from a Los Angeles number? Are you just living it up?"

"No, I used frequent flier miles and borrowed my girlfriend's cell. She's from Los Angeles."

"I can't believe you. I never could. This sucks," Jackson said.

"What?"

"I'm sorry, Maggie. It's over."

"But don't you want to—"

"No. You know, the funny thing is I thought I was happy with you all those years, and maybe I was. But you're not happy with me. You're always trying to make me into something I'm not."

Her face flushed. "What are you talking about?"

"That whole issue of me being predictable. A lot of women would find that attractive. It's not a fault."

"I know. I miss it. Really, I do!" Her eyes filled with tears, but he couldn't be sure if they were fake—and he wasn't living like that anymore. He'd been wrong in wanting her back. She would only break his heart again.

"I can't trust you anymore, Mag," he said softly. "It's gone. I'm sorry. I can't do it."

"Jackson, you're throwing us away?" She clutched his shirt. "I love you. We have a son together."

He tried not to listen to her words, to push them aside. They didn't mean anything. They were just words after all, even those about his son. Because after all these years, he knew Maggie. And how could he stay married to someone he couldn't trust? He needed to get away from her—now. He hobbled around to get his suitcase out of the backseat of Maggie's car, and as he drew it out, the letterhead of his credit union caught his attention.

"What's this?" he asked, picking up several papers from the floor of the car, scanning it. Blood swooshed through his head. "Austin's trust is empty. Do you know anything about this?"

Maggie leaned near him, trying to grab the papers. Unsuccessful, she climbed out of the car and walked around to the cement sidewalk. She stretched to get the papers from him, but he held them out of her reach.

"What's the meaning of this? Austin's trust shouldn't be empty!" He knew he was yelling, and people in the parking lot were glancing his way. He didn't care. He wanted an answer, and he wanted it now.

"I've been meaning to talk to you about this." She stopped trying to grab the papers. "There's just never been enough time to go into all the details. You see, this whole thing is kind of complicated . . ."

"I'm waiting," he said. "There's plenty of time right now."

She cleared her throat. "Do you want to go to the hospital cafeteria to talk about it? We could grab a cup of hot chocolate?"

"Maggie, tell me what you've done."

"Nothing bad, I promise. I invested Austin's trust in this incredible deal."

"What?" He adjusted his crutches. "How could you? You needed my signature to do that."

"It was a really good deal, Jaxy."

He looked at the date on the papers. "You did this when I was in the hospital with my mom."

"It's a sure thing," Maggie continued as though he hadn't said anything. "We're going to double his money."

"Don't you think that should be Austin's choice?"

"Yeah, yeah. He'll thank us for doing this. You'll see." She smoothed back some hair that had blown into her eyes.

"Us?" Jackson shook his head. "I had nothing to do with this. His trust is empty. He needs that money to go to school. Like soon—in a couple of weeks. Did you ever think about that? Did you? What's he going to say when all his money is gone, stolen by his *mother* who is supposed to protect him? This will crush him."

"I know," she said weakly. "That's why I was hoping you'd lend me the money to cover what I've taken out. Just until the deal comes through. Austin's in such a delicate state right now from all our fighting. I'm worried this will push him over the edge."

"Why don't you just take it out of the investment?"

"I can't."

"Why not?"

"Just can't."

A sick sensation pierced his stomach. "There is no investment, is there?"

"Yes, there—"

"Stop." He held up a hand. "I can't trust you, and I can't trust anything that comes out of your mouth. I don't know why I am even standing here listening to this." He turned carefully on his crutches and headed back to the waiting room.

She called after him, "But what about our son? You're not going to tell him that his money is gone and he can't go to college, are you?

Jackson, you can't do that. It would ruin him. At least lend *him* the money."

Jackson manipulated his crutches until he couldn't see her green eyes. "You just don't get it, do you? I haven't been earning much, so I don't have money just floating around. I wish I did."

"Then will you take out a loan? Please, Jaxy. We have to do something about this. We can't just sit back and do nothing while our son's life is ruined."

"You are, not we. You chose to do this." He was finished talking to her. Any more chatter would amount to no good. He wobbled into the hospital and looked out the glass doors just in time to see Maggie throw his suitcase into the gutter.

CHAPTER TWELVE

Camille woke knowing Jackson should be heading back to Island Park. He'd be released from the hospital, and what would be more romantic than enjoying God's favorite country with your beautiful wife? Nausea stirred her stomach, and the depression that had crept up on her during the drive to the cabin now proliferated inside her soul. She had to rid herself of all thoughts of him, her, them. "Darlene," she called up the stairs. "Let's go to Yellowstone. There's so much I want to see."

After squelching protests from Darlene, Camille focused her attention on packing her purse for the day trip. Then she drove up the twisting dirt road leading away from the cabin, thick branches brushing the car as Darlene sat quietly at her side. In the stillness, images of him, her, them trickled in again, flushing her with embarrassment. She had served as the bridge that carried Jackson and Maggie back to each other. A simple, trodden-on, but needed, bridge. Without her, Jackson wouldn't have had his rebound, and Maggie wouldn't have had her jealousy stirred.

"What would you like to see today?" she asked Darlene in a fake cheerful voice. To add to the act, she smiled, a tight-lipped crack of a grin, which she hoped showed motherly love.

Darlene shrugged.

"Then we're going to see the Madison River. I read about it last night. Did you know Lewis and Clark named it?"

"I didn't," Darlene said with a bored tone.

"Yep, they named it in the earlier eighteen hundred's after James Madison. He wasn't the president at that time. He was the Secretary of State."

Darlene yawned. "He probably had some political scheme going with Lewis and Clark, and that was their way of paying the soon-to-be president for scratching their back."

"That could be." Camille relaxed as the discussion bloomed into a healthy flow. She continued with her travelogue. "After the Madison River, which we'll see as we enter, I want to go to Firehole Falls. I hear it's quite a sight."

"We should see Old Faithful too, so we can say we did."

"This should be fun. Just us girls."

"I can't believe it."

"What?" Camille asked.

"Jackson seemed like a nice guy, and he turned out to be such a jerk. I mean, Austin told me, but a part of me didn't want to believe. You guys seemed to get along so well."

That one comment shattered the illusion Camille had tried so hard to construct. Lifting her arms to the steering wheel and pressing the gas pedal with her foot suddenly became a burdensome challenge. "He's hurt," Camille told her. "That kind of loss . . . it's really hard." She didn't blame him. Not really.

The sun journeyed high in the sky, casting golden rays over the land. Mother and daughter watched the Madison River snake around the countryside with brown cattails dotting the banks. Camille pulled to the side of the road, consulted the map, then headed for Firehole.

"There's a lot of lodge pine around here," Darlene said.

This statement gave Camille the perfect excuse to bring up something she'd wanted to discuss. "You know, Darlene, I've noticed since we got here that you're most passionate when you're talking about wildlife and forest preservation. You have a genuine interest, and you should learn more about what you like." Camille hesitated before rushing on. "That's why I sent off to that Yellowstone school for an application and information."

"What—"

"You told me the reason you dislike school is because you hate being told what you should learn."

"Going to the Yellowstone school isn't going to change that." Darlene crossed her arms over her chest.

"It would. Those classes are a lot more hands-on than your typical class. That should grant you the freedom you want." She stopped talking and waited. Darlene didn't say a word. "Well?"

"Well what?"

"What do you think? I'm sure there are lots of jobs you could do. Working for the government, being a teacher."

"I'm *not* you, Mom."

"Of course not. I would never want you to be."

"That's not true," Darlene muttered.

Startled, Camille looked over at her. Her daughter's face was filled with anger and, under that, hurt. "If you didn't want me to be you, you wouldn't be pushing so hard to get me to college. Choosing not to go to college isn't a crime. It's not like I've chosen to get high on drugs or kill someone. If you don't see me as you, then why do you worry so much that I'm going to make the same mistakes as you? Why do you go tense and quiet every time a boy's around? I know what you're thinking. I'm not stupid. I know you're comparing every date I bring home to Dad. You're always wondering if I fall for this guy or that guy, are they going to hurt me like Dad hurt you. I know all these things, Mom, without you ever having to say a word. You're good, Mom. Real good at getting your thoughts across. I'm not perfect and I'll make mistakes. Heck, I might even marry the wrong guy and end up divorced, but it's my life and it's my choice to take those risks."

"But—" Camille tried to interrupt.

"Mom, I know you're going to say divorce is awful. And you're right, but it's not the end. You have proven that. You showed me what a strong woman does when faced with a difficult situation. You face the fight head-on."

Camille thought about what Darlene said. Her baby was growing up, and maybe it was time to let her go just a little. Her thoughts weren't interrupted until Darlene pointed at a sign leading to the Firehole.

Camille breathed deeply when she climbed out of the car. She walked over the dirt path going to the falls. Rocks jutted from the mountain grandeur as the white rapids tumbled off the ledge, and the roar of the water filled the chilly area, the fresh air full of mist. So beautiful. This whole land was bursting with wonder—and Lewis and Clark missed it because they didn't want to go the distance. This thought, the principle of it, echoed through her, stewing until she realized she hadn't gone the distance either. She had failed to do that with Adam. His parting complaint had been he didn't know her. They were two strangers instead of lovers, and the distance between them had grown over the years.

She watched the tumbling water as it leapt over the ledge. Darlene was wrong about her. She'd never faced difficult situations head-on. How many times had she not taken the plunge and exposed her feelings? Countless. Would her relationship with Adam have been different if she had opened up? She hated the truth behind that question because she knew it would have made a huge difference. She climbed a boulder alongside the embankment and sat. This was the first time she'd ever considered that she had any fault in their marriage. There were probably more things she'd done, but she didn't have the courage to admit what they were. She wiped the tears slipping down her cheeks. Then she realized that if her relationship with Jackson had worked out, she would be guilty of keeping him and Maggie from going the distance. They still had willing hearts. They could still make it. They needed to make it. It was the right thing.

———

Jackson had the taxi make one stop at Camille's cabin before continuing on to his cabin. The ride was one hefty fare, but it was worth every cent to get away from Maggie. Besides, he needed to clear his head and consider what to do next. Painfully, he struggled to get in his back door. Austin was nowhere to be seen. Jackson hadn't been able to get hold of him on his cell phone, but the friends he'd called said they had lent Austin a vehicle and believed he was heading back to Island Park. Thankfully, the taxi driver had taken Jackson's suitcase and placed it on the porch.

The snow had melted for the most part, but the smell of more snow hung in the air around him. He had planned to spend the winter months cross-country skiing, snowmobiling, and taking pictures for the magazine. Now, with his leg zapped, those plans floated away. If he couldn't get out, life would be miserable.

A flash of Camille's smile popped into his mind. Maybe if she hadn't run back to her home, they could spend some time together. Maybe she'd forgive him for being such an idiot about Maggie. Then he remembered Darlene's accusations and the painful hurt that laced through her words when she'd spoken of Maggie. Maybe it was already too late for them.

He unlocked the door and swung himself in. He needed to rest.

———

The Britains pulled into their driveway late that evening. The trek home had been quiet but enjoyable, although both were soaked from another surprise snowstorm. They were out of the car when Camille noticed a paper taped to the cabin door, flapping in the wind. Darlene rushed past her, straight for the paper. "It's stapled and is addressed to you," her daughter said, handing it to her.

Camille took it, then fussed with her keys to get inside. She proceeded to make a fire like Jackson had taught her. Small flames quivered before they jumped to life.

"Open the letter," Darlene said.

Camille swallowed. The penmanship was small. It read:

Dear Camille,

I've made a terrible mistake going with Maggie. Will you ever forgive me? If so, please come and visit me at my cabin. I'd like to renew our friendship.

Jackson

She read the note two more times, then wadded it up and threw it in the fire. Was Maggie telling the truth that *she*, Camille, was preventing them from fixing their relationship? Those kisses she'd seen them share in the hospital when no one else was around seemed to support Maggie's claim. But Jackson's note didn't make it sound like that at all.

———

Excruciating agony stopped Jackson from doing anything except collapsing onto the nearest couch in the living room. He stayed there, not moving, except for unconscious twitches, which caused sharp intakes of breath. He had grown hungry hours before but lacked the willingness to inflict himself with the suffering necessary to prepare a bite to eat. He opted to wait for his son to return. The wait grew increasing more frustrating the later it became. At 10:13 p.m. the door made the much-wanted clicking sound. "Hey, buddy," Jackson called out. "What took you so long to get here?"

Austin shut the door and busied himself shedding his coat and boots. "Why does it matter?"

"Well I'm stuck here on the couch, as you can see, and it would be nice to eat sometime."

"What? I thought Mom was taking care of you. Isn't that her job? I thought you two were . . ."

Jackson shook his head.

"Why?"

"I couldn't go there again with her," Jackson said. "Grab me some food and let's talk."

"But Dad—" Austin went to the cupboard, snatched a box of crackers, and tossed it. The snack landed an inch away from the couch.

Jackson winced as he stretched down to grab the box. He pointed to the chair straight across from him.

"Why?"

Jackson gave him the father-stare-down until Austin relented and sat.

"In order for there to be a marriage, there must be trust, and that's gone," he told his son.

"Mom came back. She wants to change."

"Did she tell you that?"

"No." Austin seemed to shrink. "Are you going to start seeing that Camille lady?"

"What does that have to do with anything?"

"You shouldn't have been dating her while you were hoping to get back with Mom. That's probably what messed everything up." There was a note of resentment in his voice.

"Camille has nothing to do with it. This is between your mother and me."

"Well, you sure jumped at the opportunity to be alone with Camille."

"I like Camille a lot. It's been great to talk with someone who can understand what I went through when your mother left me."

His son let out a big puff of air. "Whatever."

———

Early the next morning, Camille had just cracked three eggs into a hot skillet when she heard a knock at the door. She pulled the skillet off the stove, tied the belt of her robe tighter, and answered the door. To her surprise, Jackson stood in the doorway, his head lowered, and his arms wrapped around his crutches.

"Ohhh," she said.

"Hi," he mumbled, looking faint and weak.

Leaning into the door, Camille whispered, "What are you doing here? Didn't the doctor say you were supposed to be down for the next two months?"

"Mr. Westguard was kind enough to help me." He nodded toward Mr. Westguard, who sat on a rusty tractor a couple of yards away.

"You came by tractor?" Camille said. "Oh, what am I thinking. Come in and let's get you off your leg." She opened the door and rushed to move anything remotely in his path. When he lowered himself onto the couch, she stood with cushions in hands. "Lie down so I can prop up your leg."

"That's all right," he said. "I want to sit up, but one pillow would be nice."

She helped him get situated before sitting in the chair kitty-corner from him, waiting for what he might say. She thought of the note she'd thrown into the fire, and her heart thudded painfully in her chest.

"I need to . . . um . . . I need to talk to someone."

"All right." She settled in her chair, taking the pose she usually opted for when one of her students came to negotiate about a grade. "I don't understand. Why didn't you talk to Mr. Westguard? He's a guy, after all. He'd probably understands your problem better than me."

"Camille, I don't know how to say this, but Mr. Westguard is a happily married man. He doesn't understand the problems that go along with divorce."

"I wouldn't call myself an expert in that area either," Camille said, shifting weight in her chair, "unless you want to know how to goof up."

"Would you give yourself credit and let me talk to you? I need some perspective, and I trust yours. Besides, I don't know anyone else I'd feel comfortable talking with about such personal matters."

He seemed to watch her carefully, so she tried to put on a compassionate face. It was hard to do when she kept thinking about Maggie kissing him and how she wanted to be the one doing that. "It's about Maggie—"

A jolt shot through Camille. How could he come to *her* to talk about his wife? "I know it seems strange to come to you with this, but I really don't know what to do."

"About what exactly?" Her throat felt tight.

"Well, you see, I have this problem . . ."

He seemed to be searching for the best way to explain. "Just blurt it out," she prodded.

"Fine. Before Austin's grandma, my mom, died, she set up a trust for Austin to help him with his college and to get started in life. Before we got all the paperwork done, my mother went into the hospital with ovarian cancer. She wanted the trust to be in place before her passing. I was so caught up in helping her get through chemo and keeping my job that I asked Maggie to get it arranged with both our names as custodial guardians. She had me sign papers, and I trusted her."

"You mean you didn't read them?"

"I was so exhausted."

"Besides, she was your wife, and why would you have any reason to doubt her intentions?"

His gaze connected with hers. He looked at her a long time before saying, "Yeah."

"What happened with the trust?"

"I'm not sure," he said, their eye connection lost, "but I found out yesterday that the money is all gone."

"How?"

"I don't really know. She says she put it in an ironclad investment that is going to make us all a ton of money."

"But you don't believe her?"

"She always says things like that. It's hard to put any merit in her words. When she wraps her hands around a dime, it's gone forever. Once she filled out a credit card application on the Internet in my name and spent a fortune before I ever knew about it. It took me forever to pay off."

"What did she buy?"

"Clothes, makeup, bathroom salts, furniture, girl stuff."

"It's illegal to do that."

"Yeah, I know."

"Did she help you pay it off?"

He laughed hard. "McDonald's would go out of business before that would ever happen." He ran his hand through his curls. "It's okay that she took my money, but it's not okay to take my son's."

"What? Why is what she did okay to do to you and not your son?" Anger rolled through Camille on his behalf. "Let me get this straight. She goes on the shopping binge of a lifetime, using your good name, and you have to work for years to pay it off? She basically enjoys all the loot and you do all the work." Camille waited for him to answer. When it was apparent he wasn't going to, she spoke to him in a soft, low voice. "I fell into a codependent-rescuer trap for years also. It's rough and exhausting to try to save people from themselves with not so much as a thank you. Actually, my husband kept doing the same stupid things over and over and I kept cleaning up his messes."

Jackson nodded.

"What I didn't notice while I was in the middle of it," she continued, "was that the problem kept growing bigger. I didn't realize that by doing the nice thing and cleaning up after him, I wasn't helping. I made it possible for him to keep up his bad behavior and, if that wasn't bad enough, I was losing myself in the process. I knew what he was thinking and doing, I knew what he wanted me to do, but I had no idea what I was thinking, feeling, or needing. I was so caught up in his life, I had almost completely given up mine. And then he left *me* because he felt he didn't know me. Well, I didn't even know myself."

"But you don't understand," he protested, adjusting himself to sit higher on the couch, "Austin needs that money. It will crush him—"

"What is she after?"

"Say again?"

"What does she want you to do? How does she plan for you to save her?"

"Replace the money in the trust as he needs it, so he won't know it's gone."

"He'll be cheated of the interest," she said.

"What would you do?"

"Stop saving her. Let her feel the consequences of her actions."

"You mean bring it out in the open?"

"Why not? Maggie has no problem using the information against you whenever she wants."

"But Austin. It will affect his future. Besides, what am I supposed to do? Tell him his mom stole his money?"

"I'm not telling you what to do. You just asked me what I would do."

"But—"

"I'm not saying it's easy. I'm saying it will be the best thing. It will help Maggie be accountable for what she's done. She won't stop what she's doing if you always bail her out." She stood. "Would you like a drink?"

"Uh, sure."

When she returned from the kitchen after grabbing two pops, he took one and drank deeply. After he finished, he said, "Did you get my note?"

She twisted her fingers. "Did."

"Well?"

She cleared her throat, where hundreds of short prickles of pain jabbed her lungs. "I'm not going to serve as an obstacle."

"It's not going to work with her. But you, Camille . . . you . . . you have the ability to understand." He looked at her, eyes full of tenderness, vulnerability, and affection.

"Oh, don't do this," she said. "You belong with her, and she's willing to work it out. I can't come between you." Tears filled her voice.

"But—" His brown, pleading eyes glistened.

She stood and walked out of the room.

———

After two days of storming around the house on his crutches, Jackson admitted perhaps Austin and Camille were right. He needed to forgive Maggie for what she had done. He searched deep inside until he crashed into a cement block of anger. Maggie had betrayed him. He had been a good husband, but she, with a wave of her hand, had dismissed him. "How can I forgive her?" He paused, clenching his jaw. "I'll find a way." But to what extent? That was the real issue.

More long, slow days passed. Jackson's leg ached. His son withdrew into silence, leaving Jackson to his thoughts. Camille and Austin, both good people, thought he should focus on his relationship with Maggie, but she had stolen Austin's money, the money that was his son's future. She gave no accounting for what she had done with the money. That had been the theme throughout their whole marriage— no accountability.

Where did all the money go? That was the message he had emailed her, since he wasn't sure where she had gone. Every couple of hours he checked the computer mailbox, but nothing came until the third afternoon.

He read the short note and everything became clear to him. He sent off a response, which came back immediately. He answered it again, but this time there was no reply, and he hadn't expected one. He printed off the entire conversation and asked Austin to take him for a drive in their car he'd rented so Austin could return the one he'd borrowed from his friends.

Once they were driving, Austin asked, "Where to?"

"Camille's."

"I should've known," Austin whispered between gritted teeth.

"Pull over."

"Why?" Austin questioned.

"Just do it. We need to talk."

His son sighed, steering the car off the plowed road and into the muddy snow. The Ford jerked to a halt. Austin gave him an irritated look before asking, "What do we need to talk about?"

Jackson wished he could wait until Austin found himself in a better mood before he told his boy what he had to say, but he couldn't put it off any longer. He knew that. "Son, I don't know how to say this, so I will say it flat out. Your mom came to visit me, not because she wanted to get back together but to—"

"Yes, she did. I know—"

"Will you please hear me out? Then you can say anything you want."

Austin folded his arms and pressed his lips together. At least he was quiet. Taking another deep breath, Jackson tried again. "Your mother wanted me to help bail her out of another financial problem she found herself in. You know how she likes to spend?"

Austin said nothing but kept looking through the windshield with a clenched jaw. "Well anyway, your mom has formed a nasty addiction to spending money, and I have always jumped in like your local Superman. But this time . . . this time I can't. She needs to be held accountable for her own actions."

"What's your point?" Austin asked.

"Your trust fund—from Grandma—it's gone."

"Gone?" Austin looked at him now, his face turning pale. "What do you mean? What happened to my money?"

Jackson swallowed the lump in his throat. "Your mom spent it all."

"What? How? You're lying. She wouldn't . . ." Austin stopped, obviously realizing that Maggie would. "How am I going to go . . . I need that money! Now my whole freaking future is blown up. What am I supposed to do?"

"I know this is hard." Jackson reached over to comfort him.

Austin jerked away. "What do you know? You're just blaming this all on Mom. I don't believe you."

"Whether you believe this or not, I am going to help you get your education. I should have known better. I knew she was untrustworthy with money."

"How are you going to get enough money?"

"For starters, I'm going back to Denver and getting my old job back. I figure I can earn enough to pay for your tuition, semester by semester. We'll work this out, you'll see." Austin listened. "I'm really sorry. I had no idea she would go after your money. What belonged to others, yeah, but I didn't think she would do this to you."

"This is the lowest, the meanest . . ." Austin's voice trailed off in frustration.

"Son, I know this is tough, but try not to be too hard on her. She expected me to pull my weight and play the part of rescuer like I've always done, but this time I am not going to play along. It's going to be a real surprise for her. Austin, whatever you decide to do is up to you. I'm not going to hold you hostage with the money. I'll pay you every semester whenever you go to school, and I will even figure the interest you would've earned and pay that to you too."

———

While Austin waited in the car, Jackson knocked on Camille's door. Darlene answered, a scowl coming to her face when she saw who it was. "Is your mother home?" Jackson asked.

"She's not available." She started to close the door.

He held out his hand. "Come on. Please don't do that."

She flipped her head back and glared. "And why not?"

"I need to talk to her."

"That's not good enough. Don't you think you've done enough damage?"

"But I've got to show her this." He held up the printed email.

"I'll take it." She grabbed the paper then slammed the door. The click of the lock echoed.

———

Darlene went to the drapes to peek out the window. "Mom, they're still out there. Should I ask them to leave?"

"No." Camille's head throbbed even as her fingers tried to rub the tension from her forehead. The throb had begun the instant she'd heard Jackson's voice. Why wouldn't he leave her alone?

"Are you sure you don't want to read this?" her daughter asked, waving the paper Jackson had given her.

"I'm not sure of anything. Here, let me see it."

"If it's going to make you soft on him again, then I shouldn't let you."

"I'm not going to get soft. Give it."

"Maybe I should censor it?"

"I'll be fine." She snatched the note and sat on the sofa to read it. Not a letter this time, but a series of emails. She started at the bottom of the page to follow the conversation.

Dear Jackson,

I was so glad to hear from you. I'm glad you are willing to forgive me.

Camille swallowed. Was Jackson rubbing his relationship with Maggie into her face?

Can you mail me a check to put in Austin's trust today? I promise you won't regret it. I still want to work things out so we can be together.

Love you always,

Maggie

"I can't believe this," Camille stammered.

"What?" Darlene asked.

Camille ignored her and read Jackson's response.

Dear Maggie,

I'm glad you want to help Austin. That makes me happy. As far as the money goes, I can't do it. I made a commitment to act with complete integrity and giving you the money wouldn't be true to my convictions. You need to tell Austin what you have done. Good luck on that.

Love,

Jackson

Jackson,

If you don't give me the money, we are OVER!!!!!!!

Dear Maggie,

I'm sorry you feel that way. I think you misunderstood me. I said I'd forgive you for stealing Austin's money, but we are divorced, and I have no intention of renewing a romantic relationship with you. I've actually met someone else. Guess this is where our paths separate permanently. I wish you luck.

Jackson

Camille's heart lurched and fire ran through her veins. She ran to the window and then to the door, which she opened wide. Seeing her, Jackson struggled out of the automobile, fumbling with his crutches.

Once they were in speaking distance, she said, "Jackson." Tears slid down her face.

"I love you," he whispered. "You don't have to feel the same right now—it's enough if you just give me a chance. I promise not to rush things. I know I had a lot of fault with what happened to my marriage, but I won't make those mistakes again."

He reached for her, but she put up her hand. "Wait. Maggie had a talk with me. She said I was the other woman, that I'm the reason you wouldn't get back with her."

"Camille, no. It's a lie. Our marriage failed long before I ever met you."

Camille could see the truth in his eyes. She leaned into him, felt one of his arms go around her, the other still gripping his crutch. She looked at him and he at her with his eager, wanting eyes. Heat washed over her as his lips came down on hers.

He kissed her for a long, searching moment. Her heart pounded, her nerves sang, and she had the strange sensation that she was flying. When they finally drew breathlessly apart, "Wow," was all she could think to say.

CHAPTER THIRTEEN

The next couple of days, Jackson allowed Camille to nurse him back to health. There were few things worse than having someone wait on him. Despite that, time quickly slipped away. He had talked his editor into doing a collaborative project with Camille, featuring fall in the mountains, and Camille planned to use many of the pictures that would be in her book. All in all, things were working out nicely. But Jackson wasn't completely happy.

"What's your problem?" Camille asked at lunch.

He stared at the noodles in the stew. "The soup's missing something."

"I'll get salt." She rummaged through his cupboards. "Did you know salt is incorruptible and hence a symbol of eternity and immortal life?"

"Hmm."

"Oh, great!" she muttered.

He glanced from his bowl to see that the bag had ripped and grains of salt were slipping onto the countertop and then to the floor.

"Spilling salt is a very bad sign." Camille edged around the counter, peering at the salt closely.

Was she studying it? "What are you doing?"

She tossed a pinch of salt over her shoulder. "I'm examining the way the salt spilled."

"Why?"

She threw two more pinches of salt. "If the salt scatters in the direction of someone other than the person who spilled it, the bad luck will come to either him or a person in his family."

"If that's the case, then the salt must be coming straight at me. I have one more accident to get into." Her eyebrows furrowed. "You really believe this stuff, don't you?" Jackson asked. She avoided his eyes. "You do. Good grief. You do."

"No. I don't! Not really. But sometimes I do dwell on it. I know it's stupid."

"There's no such thing as superstition. If you believe something will go wrong, then it will. It's that simple."

Camille slapped her hand against the counter, and her fiery eyes looked straight into his. "What are you doing with me if you have such a problem with my superstition?"

"Well, I, um, well, you see, my mother was into that kind of stuff and . . ." He paused, trying to figure out his motives.

"But you don't like it." Her voice had risen, and clearly, she had become emotional. "To tell the truth, I don't like it either." She swept the salt from the counter into her hand and tossed it in the garbage. Taking a breath, she said, "There, it's gone. Let's eat."

Emotions ran through him. He knew her preoccupation with superstition shouldn't bother him as much as it did. She really didn't let it intrude in their lives, not like he'd first thought. Why did even the mention of it make him feel upset?

But he knew. Of course, he knew.

"Look," he said as she sat down across from him, soup spoon in hand. "Maggie was always trying to change me, not accepting me. Part of the reason I think I've fallen for you is because you don't try to change me. I'm definitely not going to do to you what I hated being done to me. I think my problem with superstition comes from my mom . . . and what happened with my brother." He frowned at the sympathy in her eyes. He was trying to apologize but was making a mess of it.

Her lips curved in a smile. "I can't promise that I will stop thinking about superstition, but I do know reality from make-believe." She stood and came to him, placing her arms around his neck. "You're forgiven, Jackson. I love you."

Warmth spread through him. It was the first time she'd ever said the words. He had never been so grateful for salt and superstition in his life. He pulled her head down for a kiss. "I love you too."

———

Days ran into weeks until once again it was Friday the Thirteenth. *The ultimate test,* Camille thought as she worked on her course outline, jotting down notes, telling herself not to think about the date. Austin should be arriving home from his classes and hopefully would take her moping, bored daughter off her hands. The great universe must've heard her plea because the phone rang for Darlene. Moments later, her daughter bounced into the kitchen asking if she could go out with Austin.

"Be careful, it's the thirteenth," Camille said. "I get a kiss first before you go."

"Mooooom." Darlene rolled her eyes, but she rushed to her mother's cheek, giving her a peck before dashing through the door.

She had read only a few sentences of her notes when the phone rang again. She picked it up to find Jackson on the other end.

"I can't believe you said yes," he said.

Placing her papers on the desk, Camille asked, "What?"

"I was counting on you to say no. I'm tired of being the bad guy all the time, so I thought it was your turn. Besides, it's the thirteenth. I can't believe you'd let your daughter take a risk like that."

"What are you talking about?"

"The canoe trip our kids are taking down the Snake River."

"What?"

"Yeah, I told Austin if you agreed to let Darlene go, he could."

"What?" Her voice screamed her panic.

"I thought for sure since . . ."

"It's cold outside."

"Look, it's not that big a deal. The Snake River is pretty calm and not very deep where they're going. They'll be fine."

"But your son's so reckless. I'm sorry, I don't mean any offense."

"None taken. It's true."

"Why did you call?" she asked.

"To see why you said yes. I thought maybe you'd come up with some superstitious thing against it or something. In fact, I was counting on it."

"I didn't know that's what they were up to. I was just grateful to get Darlene out of the house."

"So there's no superstition with water?" He sounded uncomfortable. Why? Then Camille remembered his brother's drowning.

"In England," she said, searching her mind, "they believed you should never wash a child's hand thoroughly until they were a year old, or they wouldn't get rich when they grew up. The only other water superstition I can think of is if two people wash their hands in the same water, they'll have something bad happen to them, unless they make a cross-sign in the water with the forefinger. Now what are the chances of Austin and Darlene doing that?"

"None," he said. She bit her lip.

"So, what's for lunch?" he asked. "You didn't forget that it's your turn today, did you?" To her surprise, he sounded better. Maybe the ridiculousness of the superstition had made him feel better. Maybe her superstition had a use after all.

"Lentil stew. It's almost ready for me to bring over."

"Great. I'm starving."

———

Darlene laughed as Austin rocked the boat from side to side. He made loud noises as if they rode on a roller coaster. "Ohohohohohoho.

181

AhAhAhAh. Ooooo." The heat of the sun pressed on her face as the gentle breeze swayed against them. It felt good to be out of the cabin, breathing the wonders of natures. Her mom would have a fit if she knew, but what she didn't know wouldn't hurt her. An icy cold wave of water splashed into the canoe, running over her hand.

"That's enough, Austin. I'm getting wet and the water's freezing." The sun had suddenly hidden behind clouds, and the sky was becoming gray.

"Party pooper."

"Am not." She flicked water at him.

He wiped his face with his shoulder. "You better watch it if you don't want to go in."

She chuckled. "You'd never."

"Wanna bet?"

"No," Darlene answered. "It's cold." She held out her cupped hand toward the sky and said, "I think it's beginning to sprinkle."

"It won't turn to anything. Throw those marshmallows this way, will ya?"

The two gobbled up the marshmallows and laughed at the mess they made forming creatures out of the final few. Both washed their hands in the water. Darlene flicked water at him. He, in turn, splashed several drops in her face. Laughing, she said, "That's enough. I'm cold."

"Ah, you ruin all the fun."

"You can have fun without risking your life, you know." She picked up a paddle and guided it through the water. "The way you're always pushing the limit, it's almost like you have a death wish."

He tipped up his chin. "Naw, just want to get it out of me before school starts. That's goin' to be a real bore."

"That's right, you're studying accounting or something? That's a real sleeper."

"Not accounting, business."

"What's the difference? Neither one fits your personality." She noticed him stiffen. He hopped to his feet and began to sway the boat.

"Sit down." She laughed nervously.

"Better watch out as this future successful businessman proves you wrong and rocks your boat."

"Austin!" Cold water splashed into the canoe.

"Don't worry. I have my life under control."

She leaned forward to scoop out the water. The weight shifted them, and the canoe tipped. She held her breath as she fell into the water.

Pressure squeezed her throat as she fought the dark water. When Darlene broke through the surface, gasping, she noticed fishermen in a boat down the stream. She glanced in the other direction and saw the icy blue sky and the grayish black water curving around the browning landscape. No sign of Austin. "AUSTIN! AUSTIN!" Nothing. All she saw was the canoe swiftly floating downstream.

"AAAusssttttiiinnnn!" Her heart pounded in a rapid, irregular pattern. Where could he be? The wind blew against her wet hair, and she shivered under its breath.

A gasp caught her attention. She spun around to find Austin panting by the canoe. He coughed roughly.

"Get to shore," she yelled, pointing to the closest side.

"Whhhhy?"

"So we don't get hypothermia," she answered, swimming. The icy water splashed against her, resisting each stroke.

She swam hard for the shoreline. She stopped to catch her breath and saw the shore was only a few strokes away. The anxiety building in her chest lessened. Soon this would be over. She pushed with a final burst of energy and reached land. Pulling herself onto shore, she caught her breath before sitting up, searching for Austin.

He flopped around weakly in the water.

She yelled, "Austin!" but he didn't respond.

———

Camille couldn't shake the spilled salt from her mind or the fact it was *The Thirteenth* as she sipped her soup. Jackson flipped through the newspaper. She decided he wouldn't notice the superstition book she'd brought along with the soup. Surely there were more superstitions about water that she couldn't remember.

"Whach'a reading?" Jackson asked.

"Nothing. Just research."

He nodded and returned to his newspaper.

She put down her book, making sure the back cover faced upward. "I needed to take a few more pictures of flowers." She began packing her purse and then asked Jackson, "Do you have any more water bottles?"

"In the pantry."

"Do you want to come with me?" She called from his pantry.

"I can't go far with these crutches."

She grabbed an extra water bottle before saying, "You could wait in the car. It might be nice for you to get out. We could check on the kids, too. Would we able to see them from the road?"

"There are several places they could be. If you really insist on checking on them, then maybe we should. But don't tell them we did."

"Fine with me."

He put down the newspaper and reached for his crutches resting on the floor next to his chair, but then he stopped, looking at her intently.

Camille looked back, growing warm from his expression, the way his eyes hungrily drank her in. "I'm going to grab some blankets in case you want to sit outside when I do the shooting," she said.

Jackson extended his hand out to her. She looked at his beckoning face and grabbed hold of his hand. "You need help up?" she asked.

"No," he whispered, his warm breath spilling over her face. "I can't wait another minute to do this." He arose and pulled her close. For a long moment, she lost herself in his arms.

After they broke apart, he made it to the counter and picked up her book. "Studying superstition, huh?"

She grabbed it from his hand. "Have a problem with it?"

"No. I'd just like to know that if a real crisis came, would you be scouring those pages for the answer?"

"Very funny." She put the book into the camera bag and slipped in two bottles of water.

Soon they were driving. The sky had darkened, and along with it Jackson's and Camille's worry for their children increased. "If you don't mind," she said, "I wouldn't mind looking for our kids now. It would help me put my anxiety to rest."

"I'm fine with that. Just follow the river and we should see them soon." It didn't take long for Jackson to give driving orders. "Back up. They haven't gotten this far down the river yet."

"Are you sure they went on this part of the river?"

"The water's too low in most other places."

Camille glanced over the twisting, slow moving water once more. No wonder the first settlers named it the Snake River. It definitely looked like one. She swung the car around. The sky released water drops. "Rain, rain go away," she muttered.

"Over there," Jackson shouted. "I see something green. It might be a boat."

She drove off the road. "This isn't good. If I had bells I could ring them and chase away all the evil spirits."

"Now's not the time for superstition. I'm going to look for our kids," Jackson said.

They parked and climbed out of the car. Jackson took off down the rocky incline on his crutches. As Camille watched him disappear over the hill, she wondered what had gotten into him. He seemed to be booking. Had he seen something? She hurried after him.

Her hair whipped into her face, momentarily blocking her sight. The approaching storm would definitely create a good mood piece for her book, but she couldn't take the time to go back to the car for the camera bag now.

When she crested the hill, she saw him climbing to his feet, obviously having fallen in his hurry. Panic filled his eyes. "The kids," he said as she reached him. "I thought I heard them. I think they're in trouble."

"What?" she asked, her throat tightening. It was then she saw a canoe in the river, empty. Men in a boat were struggling to get someone out of the water.

"Mom!"

She glanced downstream to her soaking wet daughter. "Darlene!" She raced toward her. When she came close, she noticed her bluish skin and the hard trembling. "Are you all right?"

"It's Austin. I thought he would follow, but he didn't. The undercurrent must have gotten him. I have to save him."

"No, you're not. You're freezing!"

"I have to." She broke her mother's grasp.

"Darlene! Someone's already with him. We have to get you out of those clothes and warm you up."

"IIII'mmm fine," Darlene said as if drugged. "Where is Richard?"

"Your brother isn't here. Come on, you're shaking so bad."

"I'm warm. Realllly. Hot as a fiiiiirre."

Camille put her arm around her daughter and walked to where she last saw Jackson.

He balanced on his crutches, his skin losing color. "Billy," he whispered.

"Billy, your brother?" Camille asked.

He nodded.

"Did they get Austin?"

"Fishermen are bringing him."

The boat neared the shore carrying Austin's inert body.

"I'm getting the blankets," Camille announced as she edged Darlene onto a rock. "Stay," she said to her protesting daughter. She dashed to the car, her heart hurting, making her wish she were in better shape. Seconds later she returned, wrapped the blanket around her daughter, and offered one to the fishermen.

"They need to get to a hospital," one of the rescuers said.

"Billy." Jackson's face held a blank stare.

"Jackson!" Camille yelled. "Snap out of it. Your son needs you."

He gave a startled look. "What?"

"Get your son in the car." Camille pointed to the vehicle.

He nodded.

"Where's the closest hospital?" she asked one of the rescuers.

"Rexburg."

The other fisherman said, "I'd call ahead so they can warm the rooms in case they have hypothermia. Do you have a cell phone?"

Jackson nodded.

"If you have any warm liquid, get it into them. Get them there as soon as you can, before this young fellow loses consciousness."

The fishermen helped Darlene, Austin, and Jackson into the car. Darlene sat in front with Camille as Austin lay over his father's lap. Camille tended to Darlene, removing her wet clothes. Her skin had a damp chill. Wrapping a blanket around her daughter and making her sip from the water bottle was all she could think of doing. Jackson and the other men did the same for Austin, but he was unable to swallow, so they didn't force him.

As Camille sped to the hospital, she couldn't rid her mind of how foolish she had been, wanting to buy bells when her daughter and Austin were in the river, freezing. It would only have been a matter of minutes before Austin fell unconscious—not that he looked good now. And Darlene was acting drunk. They drove in silence, except for Camille telling Darlene to drink more water. When they arrived at the hospital, paramedics met the car and ordered Jackson to move slowly out from under his son. They slipped Austin onto a gurney, then put an oxygen mask over his mouth.

"Skin's cold. Pupils dilated." One of the ER nurses grabbed his wrist. "Pulse is weak. Slow respiration. Gotta move, folks." The medical team dashed into the hospital.

Camille and Darlene followed. A nurse took Darlene's medical history after handing her a cup of hot chocolate and wrapping her in a heated blanket.

———

Throughout the ordeal, Austin knew what happened around him. People talking in authoritative, hurried voices. Someone had hypothermia, but he was too tired to figure out who until he heard his dad praying. Was he dying? Was he ready? He hadn't forgiven his mom. His mom! He pictured her smiling as she winked at him. Emotion choked him. He loved her. Why had he wasted precious time? He'd put Darlene in danger, too. Was she all right? *Please, let her be all right.*

After several hours of warming his body, Austin regained consciousness. He looked at his dad and blinked. "Dad."

"Yeah, son?"

"I'm not going to business school."

"Let's not talk about that now. You're delirious. We'll have plenty of time later."

"I've decided I'm going to be a ranger."

"Are you aware you almost drowned?"

"Oh, yeah. Is Darlene all right?"

"Yes, she'll be fine. You had the worst of it."

"Good. Tell her she's going to go to school with me. We can work on the environment together."

"I will."

"Um, Dad?"

"Yes."

"I need to talk to Mom. Right now."

"Austin, what has gotten into you?"

"I was close to death, Dad." Austin closed his eyes. "I'm not ready. I need to patch things up with Mom and maybe help preserve the planet before I go. My life needs to be worth something."

————

Half an hour later, Jackson found Camille in the waiting room, crying. He pulled her into his arms as she rested her head against him like a sobbing child. "I was so stupid! I almost got our kids killed! How could I do such a thing?" The unguarded tears poured out in remorse.

"There now." He ran his hand through her hair.

"Why aren't you yelling at me?" Camille wiped at her tears. "You hate my superstition stuff. Why don't you leave me?"

"Because with superstition or without, I love you."

"Why?"

"I don't know. Sometimes you're like a vulnerable child, and yet you're independent, strong. And you bring out trust in others. Even if you live your life by superstition. At least I can learn the rules and live with you."

Camille grabbed Jackson's neck, pulled his head toward her, and kissed him hard. "Thank you for calling me independent. You don't realize how much that means. I came to Island Park to find my former independent self, and you helped me do that."

Jackson leaned over and gently tipped her chin up so she stared at him head-on. "I'm sorry I froze back there. Back at the river."

"Don't worry about that. Please don't. Anyone could've done the same under the circumstances." She gave him a crooked grin. "It is Friday the Thirteenth after all."

Jackson pulled her closer. "I need you, Camille. I need you with me all the time. I know I said I wouldn't rush you, but let's get married right away. As soon as we can."

She glanced at the tiled floor then up at Jackson. Her heart was doing funny jumps in her chest. "Okay," she said. "I'll marry you. But first I want to redecorate your cabin. That cowboy style has gotta go."

———

It took a while for the acorns to arrive in the mail, but when they did, Camille didn't hesitate for a second to fill her bucket with water. There was an old superstition that if a person wanted to know if they would be happily married to their love, they'd fill a basin with water, name the acorns—one after themselves and the other after the person they desired, then drop them into the pail. If the corns floated together, all would turn out perfect. If not, the lover would turn out to be faithless, or some other thing would happen to stop the marriage.

Camille held the acorns up. One was slightly smaller than the other. "Camille," she named one, tossing it in the bucket. It floated beautifully. Gripping the other one, she twisted it around in the palm of her hand. Bringing her clenched fist to her heart, she bent down and kissed the cool skin of the acorn. "Jackson," she whispered. Then she looked away and dropped it in the pail.

"What are you doing?"

She darted a look at Jackson strolling into her kitchen. "Nothin'," she said, not daring to look at the acorn's fate.

Jackson stood, smiling. "Camille?"

"Yes?" she asked, her pulse racing.

He knelt down, his boots making a thud against the floor. "Will you marry me?"

She giggled. "You silly man, I already answered."

"Yes, but this time I have this." He held out a ring box, opening it to show her a gold band with a square carat diamond glistening in the light with a few smaller diamonds highlighted underneath.

"It's beautiful!"

His eyes stared into hers. "Can I take that for a yes?"

She giggled again. "Jackson, stand up."

He stood inches away from her. Camille swallowed a lump of nerves and studied the powerful man who leaned toward her. He wrapped his arms around her and pulled her tightly to his chest. She could feel his warm breath spill over her as goose bumps raced through her body. His warm lips sought hers. She relished the touch and returned the kiss before pulling away.

She glanced down to see both acorns floating. "At last," she whispered before reaching up and pulling him in for another passionate kiss.

For once superstition was going her way.

We hope you have enjoyed *The Superstitious Romance* by Anastasia Alexander. Please consider telling your friends or posting a short review

Read the next novel in the Millionaire Romance Series: https://amzn.to/39sQUWr

Can love survive the world watching?

Recently divorced, Maggie Chambers just got kicked out of her apartment and has nowhere to go. Her best friend suggests that Maggie goes on a reality TV show to compete for handsome cowboy JT Devonshire's heart against the world's best women.

Having the world watch their every move, Maggie and JT learn about themselves, their past romantic wounds, and about each other—which might threaten not only their love but the show's promised happily ever after ending.

Romancing JT is a story about a lost woman searching to remake herself, a widower who is not sure if he can recover from his past, and a force that just might prove to the world that love is worth struggling for.

"Anastasia Alexander weaves an interesting story with characters that readers will love. This is a story with great emotional and psychological depth. Anastasia Alexander succeeds in keeping the excitement of her readers high while building on characters that they can easily connect to. This is, indeed, an engaging and entertaining read." -- Romuald Dzemo, Readers' Favorite

Romantic Rants Newsletter
and receive an ebook *Husband Shopping,* which explores what we can learn from reality tv on how to attract a man.

Sign Up…

Romantic Rants Newsletter

and receive an ebook *Husband Shopping,* which explores what we can learn from reality tv on how to attract a man.

https://www.authoranastasiaalexander.com/

AFTERWORD

We hope you have enjoyed *The Superstitious Romance* by Anastasia Alexander. Please consider telling your friends or posting a short review

Read the next novel in the Millionaire Romance Series

Can love survive the world watching?

Recently divorced, Maggie Chambers just got kicked out of her apartment and has nowhere to go. Her best friend suggests that Maggie goes on a reality TV show to compete for handsome cowboy JT Devonshire's heart against the world's best women.

Having the world watch their every move, Maggie and JT learn about themselves, their past romantic wounds, and about each other—which might threaten not only their love but the show's promised happily ever after ending.

Romancing JT is a story about a lost woman searching to remake herself, a widower who is not sure if he can recover from his past, and a force that just might prove to the world that love is worth struggling for.

PRAISE FOR ANASTASIA ALEXANDER

"Anastasia Alexander weaves an interesting story with characters that readers will love. This is a story with great emotional and psychological depth. Anastasia Alexander succeeds in keeping the excitement of her readers high while building on characters that they can easily connect to. This is, indeed, an engaging and entertaining read."

- Romuald Dzemo, Readers' Favorite

BEFORE YOU GO!

Romantic Rants Newsletter

Sign Up…

and receive an ebook *Husband Shopping*, which explores what we can learn from reality tv on how to attract a man.

Sign Up Now

ABOUT THE AUTHOR

Anastasia Alexander doesn't have the answers to life's love questions. What she does know is that love in the 21st century is complex. There are no easy answers, and there are richness and juiciness in exploring all the complexity that love brings.

Her credentials are two failed marriages and a current successful marriage (fingers crossed), equaling thirty-one years of marriage and a willingness to believe that the benefits of flirting aren't dead. Since she loves her current husband too much to flirt outside of marriage, she pours her love for flirting into stories.

www.ingramcontent.com/pod-product-compliance
Lightning Source LLC
Chambersburg PA
CBHW070833120626
46556CB00002B/742